ROAD OF THE DAMNED

Life of the Dead Book 2

TONY URBAN

The life of the dead is placed in the memory of the living.

— CICERO

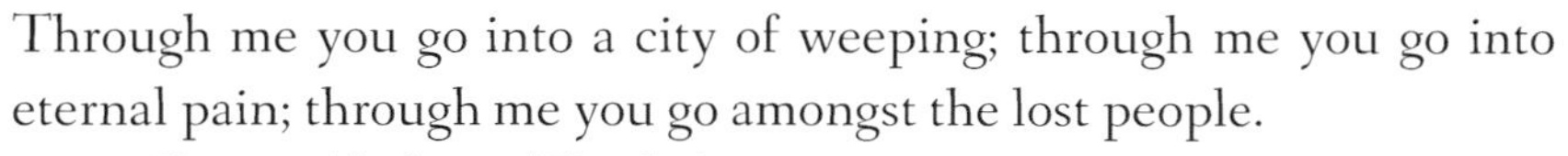

Through me you go into a city of weeping; through me you go into eternal pain; through me you go amongst the lost people.

— Dante Alighieri, The Inferno

CHAPTER ONE

Between the zombies and the wrecked cars, Wim had no way around the roadblock. He examined the map he'd earlier grabbed from a gas station and which now laid unfolded on the seat beside him. He knew there were other means of going south, but near as he could tell from the labyrinth of lines, retreating from his current location, then taking a new route would take well over an hour.

Wim wasn't worried about the time. He was in no great hurry, but he preferred to stick to the main roads. Because even though he was less than a hundred miles from his farm, he was already further away from home than he'd ever been or ever intended to be. He had liked it that way in the time before the plague. Before the zombies. Now, however, his isolation had become a terrible hindrance.

He recalled a farm he passed two miles back. Farms tended to catch his eye, and this one in particular made him more than a little sick inside. More specifically, he was jealous of the John Deere S690 Combine that stood in front of the freshly painted crimson barn.

He didn't have any combines at his farm; there had never been money for one. The Deere would have cost over four hundred thousand dollars new for the base model, and now it would do nothing but sit there, exposed to the elements and rust away. Maybe he could get a little more use out of it, if luck was on his side. The way Wim figured, he was due.

He did a u-turn in the middle of the road and retreated to the sprawling farm where the combine waited. He shut off the Bronco and exited it. Wim's pulse quickened as he approached the combine, and he imagined non-farming men would react similarly at a chance to drive a Lamborghini or Porsche. He hoped the keys would still be in the compartment, and, when he climbed into the cab, that little prayer was answered.

The combine fired up right away. It operated along the same lines as regular tractors but with a sixteen-row corn head attached, maneuvering it around proved more of a challenge than he'd expected. When he steered it onto the road, he gritted his teeth every time it crept over five miles an hour. Wim breathed a little easier when the clearing on each side of the road grew wider. Once he got rolling, he had a clear path back to the horde.

Any thoughts that might have flitted through his mind about the zombies possibly dispersing vanished when he reached the roadblock. They remained in the general vicinity of where he'd left them, with only a variance of a few feet in any given direction. The combine was anything but discreet, and the sound drew their attention well before the machine came close enough to do any damage.

Wim expected them to scatter out of the way, but instead, they came toward the sound of the tractor. Toward death, he thought, then reminded himself that they were already dead. Still, he assumed they'd move to avoid the coming fate. He thought that right up until the pointed green fangs of the corn head hit the first wave of zombies.

The machine pushed a few aside, where they stumbled and dropped off the roadway. Others became ensnared in the teeth of the combine like gristle from a steak. Wim opened up the throttle as far as it would go, and the teeth yanked the zombies further inward with violent force. There, the cutter bar began chopping away at them.

The day's peaceful, golden glow turned pink as a fine mist of blood filled the air. It splattered against the windshield of the combine, and Wim hit the wipers, which swished back and forth, back and forth in a crimson haze. He motored forward and felt bodies break, then explode under the twenty-ton weight of the combine. Wim's meager breakfast rose up his throat, but he fought it back down.

They're nothing but husks, he told himself. No different from cutting down the dead crops at the end of the season. Think of this as an extermination.

But he saw their faces as they fell before him. They might be zombies. They might be monsters. But they had been people once. When the next wave of blood turned his windshield red, he left it that way. It was easier.

Within a few minutes, he realized the big machine marched forward with ease. He'd finally mowed down the last of the zombies on the road. He hit the wipers again to verify that and saw nothing ahead of him but open road. He checked the rear mirrors and saw the river of crimson gore that flowed down the two-lane road behind him. Blood and chunks of mangled body parts blew out the unloader pipe like gory rain.

"Grain tank must be full," he muttered. He made a wide, arcing pivot in order to return to his truck.

When back at the farm from which he'd borrowed the combine, Wim hopped down from the cab. He noticed that the John Deere green paint had become camouflaged in red and regretted returning it in such unsatisfactory condition, even though the rightful owners were almost certainly dead. Heck, they might have even been amongst the group of zombies he'd run down.

When he returned to his Bronco and drove back toward town, the truck slipped and slid as he hit the gore. He slowed the vehicle down to a crawl, and the tires gained traction. Wim didn't know if it was possible to hydroplane on minced-up human beings, but he decided not to take any chances.

CHAPTER TWO

It was obvious Peduto was sick. Her throat clearing had progressed to a persistent cough and sweat dripped from her forehead. When they crossed into Delaware, Bolivar headed toward Dover, but Peduto asked if he would take her to the beach instead. He pushed aside his concerns over going AWOL, which were minor considering that Uncle Sam tried to turn them into crispy critters back in Philadelphia and did as she wished.

They bypassed the bay, where a handful of tourists and fishermen were apparently somehow unaware or unconcerned with what was happening to the north. They eventually came upon Cape Henlopen, which was deserted aside from a lone van in the lot. Instead of parking, Bolivar drove the car onto the sand, an act which drew a raised eyebrow from Peduto.

"What's the worst that could happen? They arrest us?"

She laughed. It was the first real laughter he'd heard in days, and the sound was so sweet he thought he might start crying all over again. He only stopped the car when the front tires were in the ocean. Gentle waves licked at the rubber.

They both exited the Saab, and Bolivar watched her as he

breathed in the damp, salty air. It was the longest she'd gone without coughing in some time. Peduto took off her cap and tossed it onto the wet sand. She then pulled out the bobby pins which held her bun in place and let her hair fall free. It surprised Bolivar to see a fair amount of gray intermixed with the black. Her loose curls hung halfway down her back and danced lazily in the ocean breeze.

"Will you sit with me, Bolivar?"

He nodded. "On one condition."

“What's that?"

"You call me Jorge."

She smiled, but it didn't quite reach her red, feverish eyes. "I'll try."

"Then we'll sit."

And they did. The silence was broken only by the gentle crashing of the waves and neither of them minded.

As THE SUN fell below the horizon, a cold breeze coming off the ocean replaced the warmth of the sun's golden rays. Bolivar saw Peduto shivering, and even though he suspected it was more her fever than the actual temperature, he gathered together small bits of driftwood and random debris and used a road flare to start a small bonfire.

As it crackled and popped to life, he watched Peduto as she endured another horrible coughing fit. It ended with her spitting two mouthfuls of mucous into the sand.

"Sorry. I've never been much of a lady."

Bolivar pretended not to notice as she used the back of her hand to wipe some bloody drool from the corner of her mouth. "No need to apologize."

"I wish we had some marshmallows," she said as she stared into the fire.

And he so wished he could do that for her. "That, I can't help you with. Sorry."

She shrugged her shoulders in an 'it's not important' gesture. "My parents used to take us to the beach every fall after tourist season died down. That was Myrtle Beach, though. And when my sister and I were still young, we'd all camp out on the sand most of the nights and make s'mores and tell ghost stories like the legend of Blackbeard and the ghost ships like the *Mary Celeste*. We did that every year until I was in high school and got the idea that spending time with my family was lame. Stupidity of youth and all that."

"I actually never even saw the ocean in person until I joined the Army."

"Really?"

"Yeah. I grew up in Illinois. We went to Lake Michigan once, but it rained the whole time. I don't think we even left the hotel."

"I haven't even seen my sister in four years. My mom in almost two. We keep meaning to get together, but, you know."

Bolivar nodded. He knew all too well the havoc military life played on family dynamics.

Peduto looked away. "Can I ask you a question? Are you religious?"

Bolivar thought about it, then nodded. "I was raised Catholic. I kept up with it pretty regularly until I was stationed in Iraq. But I still believe." Do I? he thought, remembering all the horror he'd seen the last few days.

"I've never read the bible. I mean, I know about most of the main events, the cliff notes, I guess you could say, but I don't know how it all works with the dying and how it's determined whether you're going north or south."

She hesitated and almost didn't go on but eventually did. "What I'm wondering now is, are you judged by the worst thing you've ever done? Like, even if you've led a mostly moral life—not perfect, that's for sure—but you were a decent person most of the time, but if you did something really, really awful, does it cancel out all the good?"

"I wouldn't think it does. In the New Testament, Christ preached forgiveness. They say anything can be forgiven if you repent. And personally, I can't imagine good people would be denied Heaven because of one bad act. Or even a handful of bad acts. That's not what I want to believe, anyway."

Peduto stared into the fire for a long while, so long that Bolivar thought the subject was closed. When she did speak again, she kept her eyes cast toward the flames.

"I was sent to Afghanistan after the Towers came down. Just south of Kandahar. We all went in there thinking we were going to find Bin Laden and stop the terrorists and all that happy horse shit. But when we got there, it didn't take long to realize that it was so far removed from reality that it wasn't funny.

"Most of the folks we came across weren't Taliban. They were a bunch of pissed-off dirt farmers. They weren't bombing cities or plotting attacks in America. They couldn't even read a map. There were small groups here and there that actually wanted to fight or plant IEDs, but most of them just wanted to be left alone. Our job was basically to train the Afghan security forces about how to be soldiers, but it was babysitting more than anything else. I became an Xbox master during downtime.

"What was really weird to me was that there were always boys around. Street kids, probably ten to fifteen or sixteen years old. And they were constantly hanging around the older Afghan men who had money. At first, I thought they were just beggars, but they never hit us up for anything, so I started to pay more attention.

"One guy in particular—we all called him 'Sultan' because he acted like he was so much better than everyone else—always had a kid with him, and the boy was usually wearing make-up. I asked one of the brass about it, and he said they were 'bacha bazi' and that it was tradition. Told me to forget about it, but I'm a woman, and you know it's next to impossible for us to forget anything.

"So, one night, I saw the two of them walking down the street, and I followed. They went into some sort of club or lounge, and I snooped around the outside until I found a window that was open wide enough to spy from. I saw the boy dancing for a group of men, dancing like a woman dances, and they were all throwing money at him. And then after that..."

She stopped again, and Bolivar saw the flames reflected in her wet, teary eyes.

"After that, the other men left. The Sultan said something to the boy, and the boy got undressed. I couldn't watch once I realized what was going on, but I waited outside, and when they left, I followed them down an alley. There was no one else around. I took out my service pistol and shot that son of a bitch in the back. He was dead before he hit the ground."

She looked at Bolivar, sobbing. "But then the kid, the boy, he was probably twelve, he ran straight at me and jumped on me. He started punching me and hitting me and trying to grab my gun. He bit my hand."

Peduto extended her hand, where a white, crescent-shaped scar dotted and dashed across the fatty flesh between her thumb and index finger like Morse code.

"And when he bit me, I jerked back, and when I did, I must've squeezed the trigger again, and the pistol went off. I shot him right in the neck, and he fell backward and the blood was running out like someone had just turned on the faucet.

"The bullet must have hit that big artery in his throat, the one vampires always drink from in the movies, and it was over before I could even move. All I could see were his big dark eyes with that perverted mascara painted around them, staring up at me as he died."

"I ran back to the base and never told anyone. The police wrote it off as a mugging gone bad or something. But, my God, I can still see his face every time I close my eyes."

Her hitching sobs led to another violent coughing spell. She gasped for air, and Bolivar rushed to her side and wrapped his arm around her. Peduto eventually stopped coughing, but when she did, she vomited up a mass of red tissue mixed with yellow phlegm. She spat several times to clear her mouth of it.

"I'm going to die. I know that, and I'm okay with it, especially considering all the shit that's going down. But please tell me I'm not gonna go to Hell for that. I was only trying to do the right thing."

He pulled her close to him. "It was an accident, Gwen. A terrible one, I'll give you that, but how many lives did you save in Afghanistan? How many times did you risk your own life these last few days to save other people? To save me, even?" He wiped the tears from her face. "If anything I was taught in church was true, God has already forgiven you. All you need to do is forgive yourself and trust him to do the rest."

She composed herself as much as possible. "Why do you think this is happening?"

Jorge waited a long while, trying to come up with an answer to the same question he'd been asking himself for days. "I don't know. I'm not sure I want to."

Gwen squeezed his hand. "Don't let me turn into one of those monsters."

"I won't. I promise."

Some time through the night, they both fell asleep, and by the time the sun peeked above the horizon, the fire had burned itself out. Bolivar could feel Peduto's body heat through her clothes and couldn't even hazard a guess at how high a fever she must be running. Her black and gray hair was soaking wet and slicked against her head. Her eyelids were swollen and inflamed. A trickle of blood ran out of the corner of her mouth, and he wiped it away with his fingertips.

She woke an hour later, and it almost seemed like she was making a turn for the better. She sat up and noticed their Saab had sunken into the sand up to its bumper.

"I hope he had flood insurance," she said and laughed. But now, her weak laugh completely lacked the joy he'd heard yesterday. Her end was close. It was evident in her voice and eyes and even the way she held herself.

"I want to feel the ocean on my feet one more time. Can you grab me a water?"

Bolivar watched her step into the ocean where the white foamy waves washed over her feet, then her ankles, then her knees.

His own bare toes sunk into the damp brown sand as he moved to the open trunk and took out the last water bottle. Tucked in the mesh netting at the side of the trunk, he spotted a construction paper art pad. He grabbed it and paged through the pastel-colored pages, where he saw stick figure dogs, horses, and families. One drawing was labeled "Mommy, Daddy, Eli, Me." Underneath Me was a small girl with sun-yellow hair.

Bolivar wondered if the girl was still alive or if she and her family were victims of the plague or the zombies. If she was alive, how long would that last? How long was anything going to last now?

The beach was empty that morning, and he knew somewhere inside that the bombings hadn't limited the chaos to Philadelphia. It couldn't be that easy. He was always skeptical about apocalyptic predictions, even the ones in the bible, but his thoughts on that were evolving. Bol thought the end was near, but he tried to push that aside as he closed the trunk and turned back to the ocean.

He saw that Peduto had collapsed into the water. He dropped the bottle and ran into the waves, his long strides kicking up liquid, but by the time he got there, she was dead.

Bolivar stood in the gray, waist-deep murkiness of the Atlantic and raised her face above the water. He reached into the holster of her waistband and took out her M1911 pistol. He wasn't even sure if it would fire after taking a swim in the ocean. He shook it out as best he could and saw there was already a round chambered, and the safety was, of course, off.

Bol pressed the barrel tight to the skin between her eyebrows and pulled the trigger. The surrounding water turned crimson.

He let the tide take her.

CHAPTER THREE

After almost ten hours of driving, Wim spotted Ramey on the road. At first, he wasn't sure. A good quarter of a mile stood between them, but the road was straight and his eyesight above average. Three vehicles had collided in the middle of the street, and she stood there amidst them.

He stopped the Bronco less than ten feet from the scene. Her back was turned toward him, and, as her body flailed, her struggle became obvious. Someone, or something, in one of the crashed cars had ahold of her arm.

"Ramey!" he yelled.

She half-turned, and when that happened, Wim realized the thing holding her arm was a zombie. As soon as her attention became diverted, it bit down on her forearm and took away a mouthful of flesh.

Wim's temporary joy disappeared in a flash. He grabbed a .38 from a holster on his belt and, in one swift move, raised and fired. The zombie that chewed on Ramey crumpled sideways, a black dot on its forehead and brains leaking from the back of its skull.

With the zombie dispatched, he ran toward the cars. Toward

Ramey. She'd fallen to her knees and clutched the wound on her arm. Blood seeped through her fingers.

"Oh, heck. You got bit." This is all my fault, he thought. I distracted her when I hollered, and that thing bit her. It was just like he thought when this mess started; he was cursed. And now he was cursing everyone around him. *Why did I ever leave the farm?*

She looked up at him. Her turquoise blue eyes pained and terrified.

And that's when he finally got a good look at her face. This wasn't Ramey.

The eyes were wrong, the lips, the skin, the age. He'd been so eager to find the girl that he assumed the first female he saw was her. But that didn't change the fact that this woman was in trouble.

"You've got to help me," she said. Her words came out rapid fire, frantic. Her eyes spilled tears. "Please, man."

Wim collected himself. This was still his fault, and he wanted to do whatever he could. But what was there to be done? "What can I do?"

"Cut it off!"

"What?"

"My arm! Cut it off!"

He thought he'd heard wrong. "What did you say?"

"Cut my fucking arm off, man! Before it's too late!"

No, he heard right the first time. "I have a machete in the truck."

"Get it!"

Wim sprinted to the Bronco and dug through the guns and ammunition in the backseat until he came across the old machete. He'd included it on a whim. He had assumed he might need it to chop at a fallen tree branch or some random menial task. Not amputate a stranger's arm. But he grabbed it nonetheless.

The woman had collapsed on the pavement by the time he got back to the wreckage. Pain riddled her face, and she rocked back and forth.

"Hurry, you asshole!"

The bite seeped blood about halfway between her wrist and elbow. He held her hand against the road and raised the machete overhead. She watched him.

"You might ought to close your eyes."

Rage filled the look she shot his way, but she did as told.

Wim swung the machete down. It sliced into her flesh two inches below the elbow. The woman shrieked. But the limb was still attached. Blood shot out from the fresh cut, and within seconds, the pavement looked like someone had dropped a gallon of red paint on the road.

He swung again, and the bone broke. A third swing finally finished it off.

Wim pulled off his flannel shirt and tore off the sleeve. He tied it off at her elbow, and the gushing blood slowed to a weak trickle. That's when he realized she'd gone unconscious.

He knelt at her side to wait and see what, if anything, would happen. As soon as he did, he heard scraping sounds against the hot asphalt.

He jumped up and found two zombies behind the wrecked cars. One, a woman in her thirties, the other a little girl with a chestnut-colored ponytail. They looked like mother and daughter. Cuts and scrapes covered their exposed skin. Wim noticed one of the vehicles, a Hyundai sedan, was missing its windshield and guessed they'd been thrown out in the wreck.

With his .38, he first shot the mother in the head. She crumpled to the ground, and the daughter looked down at the dead woman. She almost looked confused. Wim was thankful she wasn't looking at him because he shot her, too. She fell atop her mother, and both stayed down.

A few yards beyond them, a man with a crew cut crawled on his hands and knees. He came from the general direction of a black Wrangler, the third vehicle in the crash. When he caught sight of Wim, he reached out with a bloodied arm and growled. Several of his teeth had been snapped off, leaving jagged shards that looked like fangs inside his mouth. Wim shot that zombie, too.

His ears rang from all the gunshots, and he couldn't hear something move behind him. Didn't hear the dragging of feet across pavement. Didn't hear the throaty gasps that came inches from his head.

If the zombie had gone in head first and bit him, he'd have been a goner, but it grabbed him by the shoulder instead and tried to pull him close. In his shock, he stumbled a step backward, and his back pressed against a woman's soft chest. Only one hand held him, and it didn't take much of a guess to deduce the identity of his attacker.

The zombie lunged for the side of his face, but Wim turned his head just in time. The zombie hit the back of his head, jaws snapping. He felt pain as something pulled his hair, and Wim jerked himself forward. A clump of hair came out by the roots, and as he turned, he found a shock of his black locks in the woman's mouth.

She opened her jaws and her tongue pushed out as if trying to expel the hair. Wim took a few steps back. Her arm had quit bleeding entirely now that she was dead and her eyes had taken on that too familiar dull gaze. They turned to him, and, for a moment, he thought he saw anger flash.

Wim imagined he deserved her rage. Maybe she'd have been able to get away from the first zombie if he hadn't opened his big trap. Maybe she could have saved herself, but instead, he came along and sealed her fate.

Wim had no idea how many zombies he'd killed so far, but this was the first person whose actual death he had caused. He wanted to forget it. To push this incident somewhere deep inside where it could only leak out in nightmares. Perhaps, the ability to do that would come in time, but for now, the only thing he could do was kill her again. So, that's what he did.

CHAPTER FOUR

The light burned so brightly that Emory could see it with his eyes closed. So bright he wondered if it was *the* light. Before his eyes could adjust, he heard coughing, and he doubted there was coughing in Heaven.

His eyelids fluttered, then opened, and he saw he was in the backseat of a car or perhaps a van. He tried to sit up, but a deep ache in his chest put an end to that. He groaned from the pain.

"Oh, shit! Oh, shit, bro! He's a zombie!"

"Shoot him! Quick! Do it!"

The vehicle in which he was riding swerved back and forth across the road. Emory heard rummaging from the front seat and fought to catch his breath long enough to speak. The distinctive sound of a round of ammunition being chambered in a pistol was the encouragement he needed.

"I'd prefer you don't shoot me. I promise I'm harmless." He rushed the words out via a mouthful of air. Emory tried to raise his hands in surrender, only to realize he couldn't move them. He tried his legs with the same lack of results.

"You think he's okay, bro?"

"I never heard one of them talk."

"Good point."

The vehicle slowed and the tires crunched against gravel before coming to a stop. The men who occupied the front seats turned and stared at him. They wore handkerchiefs over their mouths like Wild West outlaws. The one in the passenger seat held a pistol. He looked to his friend. Both were no more than twenty years old.

"How do we know he's still human?" the one with the gun asked.

"I don't know. We have to ask him something only a real person could know. Like what's the square root of four hundred?"

"Twenty," Emory said.

"Is that right, bro?"

"I don't know."

"It's correct. I assure you." Emory glanced downward and discovered jumper cables binding his hands and feet together. "Would you gentlemen please untie me?"

The duo exchanged glances, then nodded at each other.

As they freed him, they explained to Emory how they had rescued him from the zombies near the electronics store. That had been three days ago, and Emory'd been unconscious ever since.

They told him he grabbed his chest before he passed out. After hearing that, Emory took a deep breath and felt like he'd been kicked in the sternum by a horse. He'd suffered a minor heart attack more than a decade earlier and normally carried nitroglycerin pills but had neglected to bring them along when Christopher showed up, frantic over his aunt. Remembering Christopher caused a different ache in his chest.

The bros' names were Andy and Vince, and they weren't brothers in the way Emory was familiar with. They were *Rho Iota Pi* fraternity brothers who attended the Pitt main campus in Oakland. There had been a third with them when they rescued Emory. They didn't go into much detail aside from sharing that his name was Bill and that he didn't make it.

For them, the chaos had started when another fraternity brother suddenly attacked people inside the frat house.

"Everyone he bit turned into a fucking zombie, bro!" was how it was described. Emory wasn't sure if they were calling him bro or if they were calling the zombies bros. The men escaped in the fraternity's transport van. They were fleeing the city when they saw Emory collapse in the street.

"Even though you're old, we couldn't just let you get eaten," Vince said.

"I very much appreciate that."

They'd been driving aimlessly for three days, hoping to find a place that wasn't filled with zombies, but their efforts were fruitless. Along with Pittsburgh, the cities of Cleveland, Columbus, and Harrisburg were overrun. They were debating whether to check Philadelphia or Baltimore next.

"Philly was busted even before zombies," Andy said with a laugh, and he looked to Emory. "Am I right?"

Emory didn't have a chance to answer, not that he knew the proper response, before Andy started coughing. He pulled off the handkerchief covering his mouth and spit a wad of red-tinged mucous into the grass.

"This cold sucks, bro," Andy said as he wiped his mouth with the back of his hand.

He died later that day.

THEY WERE HEADING SOUTH and had just crossed the border between Maryland and West Virginia. Andy rode shotgun, and Vince was so busy focusing on the road ahead that he didn't realize his fraternity brother was dead until he came back.

Emory saw Zombie Andy reach for Vince.

"Vincent, watch out!" Emory yelled.

Vince glanced over just in time to see Andy snarling and leaning in for a bite. He hit the brakes, and the van threatened to careen out of control as it swayed back and forth. Somehow, he kept it on the road.

Emory leaned forward and reached between Andy and the passenger side door. He grabbed the handle and shoved it open.

"Push him out!"

Vince gave Andy a hard shove, and the zombie toppled backward, tumbling head over feet out of the van. Emory watched him bounce and roll. When the momentum of the fall expended itself, Andy stood up. The fall had skinned his face to the bone, but he ambled along nevertheless.

Vince stopped the van just a few miles up the road at the outskirts of Berkeley Springs. No one, living or dead, was in sight. Vince shut off the engine and looked at Emory in the backseat. Emory noticed the boy's eyes were blood red.

"That will happen to me, too, won't it?" Vince asked.

Emory swallowed hard. He knew the answer. "I believe nothing is a certainty."

Vince pulled the handkerchief over his head, revealing thick, green snot that ran from his nostrils. His lips were chapped and raw. He used the rag to blow his nose.

"That's nice of you to say." Vince handed Emory the keys. "You take these."

He opened the door and hopped out.

"What are you doing, Vince?"

Vince flashed a goofy smile which made him look five years younger. "You try to find somewhere safe. I'm going back to find Andy. Bros for life, right?"

He extended his fist. Emory was familiar with fist bumping, thanks to Christopher, and he obliged. That made Vince's smile even bigger.

"I'm glad we saved you from the zombies."

Vince turned away and jogged along the highway.

"I am, too, Vince. I am, too."

Emory exited the backseat and climbed behind the wheel. He restarted the engine but took another look at Vince in the rearview before pulling back on the road and leaving him behind.

CHAPTER FIVE

ALMOST IMMEDIATELY, RAMEY REGRETTED LEAVING THE FARM and Wim. Not because she was scared. She was, of course. It would be insane to not be scared in what the world had become. And not because she felt helpless either.

She was no fighter, but she'd handled herself pretty well, all things considered. But she was lonely, and the quiet was wearing her down. The radio recited nothing but static, and the old pickup didn't even have a cassette player.

The steady rumble of the mud tires against the asphalt was anything but soothing. Every time she rounded a curve, she expected to drive into a crowd of zombies or slam into an abandoned car or maybe drive off a cliff. If someone else was along, she'd have a second set of eyes and someone to talk to or to listen.

The thought of turning around and driving back to the farm sounded better with each passing mile, and it was only her pride that kept her from doing just that. Well, pride and the fact that she doubted she'd be able to return to the farm without getting lost along the way.

She'd been using Stan, the now dead trucker's, map to navigate, but she'd already made her share of wrong turns. She knew she needed to go south and kept finding roads that sent her in that direction. Without the route markers, she was liable to end up back in New York if she wasn't careful. The further she drove, the more she realized finding that X on her father's map was nothing but a fool's errand.

She was tired, hungry, and felt close to breaking. And while she couldn't do anything about the latter, she hoped taking care of the first two issues might get her back on track. About twenty miles later, she spotted a roadside convenience store and pulled in.

Millions of chunks of safety glass littered the macadam in front of the shattered double doors of the entryway. Ramey felt them dig into her shoes as she walked over them. Inside, someone had dislodged and upended many of the shelves. She noticed some merchandise was missing entirely—like cigarettes and snuff—but most of the items were still in stock if you didn't mind picking them off the floor.

Ramey grabbed an assortment of candy bars from the piles and shoved a few into her pockets. She tore the wrapper off a Snickers and took a bite, then moved on to something more nutritious.

"Jackpot," she said as she spied a jumble of beef jerky under an overturned rack of magazines.

Her hands were full, though, and she moved toward the counter in search of some bags. Before she could get them, a voice from behind stopped her.

"You planning to steal all that?"

The voice was a man's and carried no humor, but she attempted a charming smile as she turned around. When she saw him, she was relieved to see he looked about her age. Three or four years older at the most.

He was scrawny but tall, and she imagined he could have been a basketball player on just about any high school team around so long as he could walk without tripping over his own feet. But he also had long, greasy hair, rings through both eyebrows and earlobes stretched to the size of fifty-cent pieces.

"Left my wallet in the truck." She kept the smile, hoping to get one in return. She did not.

"This is my store."

She thought the man looked nervous. Maybe even a little scared. Ramey was always confident in her ability to talk her way out of trouble and decided to give it a shot.

"Then shouldn't you be wearing one of those shirts that say, 'My name's Bill'?"

"It's in the laundry."

Was that a hint of a smile? She thought so. "Is it now?"

He nodded. "And it's Danny. My name, I mean."

"I'm Ramey."

Danny moved behind the counter. He pointed to a picture on the wall showing a middle-aged man holding up a plaque that read, 'Region's #1 Franchise.'

"That was my dad. Owned this place for almost twenty years. I've been working here since I was this high." He tucked his thumb into his waistband. "Even though he's gone now, I hate to see people like you tearing it apart."

She'd been wrong about the smile. If anything, the look on his face was a grimace. The skin around his eyes was a mosaic of red-purple bruises and his irises were the color of old coffee stains.

"I didn't do any damage. Just grabbed a couple candy bars. And I'll give them back if that's what you want."

She emptied the contents of her pockets onto the counter. Danny looked from them up to her face.

"Can't give back that Snickers now, can you?"

He had a point there. "I'll pay you for it, then." She rummaged through her pockets and came out with a dollar bill and some change, which she set on the counter.

Danny sneered, and when he did, his lip pulled up to reveal gray gums that leaked pus, which filled in the cracks between his teeth like grout. "Pay? With cash. You think money's worth anything now?"

While she tried to work out an answer, Danny changed the

course of the discussion by extracting a shotgun from behind the counter. He held it in his hands, cradling it like a baby.

"Listen, Danny, I'm sorry. I—"

"You listen, bitch."

He tilted the barrel in her direction, racked the shotgun, and pointed it at her face. "Drop your pants. Now!"

CHAPTER SIX

The world was quiet when Solomon regained consciousness. He thought he remembered it sounding quite different before, but his memory was only half working. He tried to sit up and couldn't.

He felt restraints holding his arms, and that brought part of the last few hours rushing back. He was in a hospital. He'd been taken there by ambulance for some reason. But he couldn't recall why.

When he attempted to move his head, it met with the same resistance as his arms. Bastards have me trussed up like a Christmas goose, he thought.

"'ello. I've come to and would appreciate a hand."

He waited but received no response. His patience was running thin.

"Are any of you wankers out there? I want loose of this fucking table." Another twenty seconds of silence passed and Solomon was done waiting.

He jerked his right arm with as much force as he could muster. The strap holding his arm gave way with a tearing sound, but the movement sent a fire-poker of pain searing through his skull. What the holy hell?

He reached up with his free hand and undid the strap holding his head still. That allowed him to sit up, but the motion of doing so made his stomach do somersaults and again made his head feel on the verge of implosion. Everything went blindingly white, and he squeezed his eyes closed to stop the brightness.

Then it all came rushing back to him. His whoring wife becoming a zombie. Killing the bint. Taking the gun into the neighborhood and seeing his ugly bird of a neighbor eating her tot. Getting ready to shoot her. And—

The gunshot.

He remembered a sudden halt after that. Some bastard shot him. Bollocks.

Solomon unfastened the strap on his left hand and climbed down from the operating table, careful to move his head as little as possible because every time he moved it, the pain multiplied. He looked around the room.

Rust-colored blood covered the floor, and his feet stuck to it like he was walking on ticky tape. Mixed in with the spilled blood were a variety of surgical instruments. That brought the rest of it back. The screams, the struggle. Zombies had overtaken the room, but they were gone now, leaving destruction in their wake.

He spied the sleeve of a surgical scrub, and when he looked closer, he realized an arm was still inside it. He kicked it out of his way, and it slithered across the floor and into an overturned bin. Goal!

Solomon spotted a mirror mounted on the wall above a small sink and stepped to it. He saw his reflection, and his eyes went to a half-inch wound on his forehead. He leaned in closer for a better look and realized it wasn't just a wound, it was an egg-shaped hole. The edges were charred black and a nub of pinkish-gray tissue poked out.

"Is that my fookin' brain?"

He reached up with his forefinger and pressed on the tissue. It felt dense and malleable like gelatin, which was still a few minutes away from being set. He kept pushing until the bit of brain tissue disappeared into the hole in his skull, but as soon as he removed his finger, it popped back out again. It reminded him of the Whack-A-Mole game he played at the arcade when he was a lad.

Saw poked it again, this time pushing until his finger was buried to the first knuckle. That made him feel so horny he would have shagged his dead wife if she'd been in the room, but he also forgot where he was. His name, too, for that matter.

His finger came out of his head with a popping noise, and he quickly recalled what was happening. He noticed another hole above his left temple. That one was larger and the surrounding skin had splayed out in a small x. Marks the spot, he thought. No brains extruded from that hole, but clear fluid seeped out.

"Better patch myself up. Don't need me brains falling out of my noggin."

He found bandages and a roll of gauze on the floor. Both were stained with the blood of the dead, but they would have to do. He covered both wounds, then wrapped the gauze around his head a few times and tied it off in a knot.

As he looked at himself again in the mirror, he thought it looked like he was wearing a ninja headband of sorts. For some reason, that made him giggle like a schoolboy.

After the laughter stopped, he pushed open the swinging door to the room, expecting to see the hallway full of zombies, but it was as empty as the operating suite. There was plenty of blood and wreckage but no bodies, living or dead.

His head still throbbed, and his priority was to find something for the pain. After some searching, he discovered a medicine cart. The damned thing was locked up tight, so he needed to find a way inside.

He slammed it against the wall several times. That added a few dings but didn't spring the drawers. He searched the hallway until he saw an ax mounted on the wall. He chuckled as he read the instructions aloud. "In case of emergency, break glass. If this ain't a fookin' emergency, I don't know what is."

He used his elbow to shatter the glass and pulled out the chunks with his hand, ignoring the multiple cuts he sustained. They were pinpricks compared with the bomb inside his head.

Saw removed the ax and returned to the cart. After five good blows, he thought he'd be better off using the rotten thing to cut off his head instead. But eventually, the locks gave way. He sifted through the bottles, trying to find names that meant something to him. He found and pocketed an antibiotic. That might come in handy considering the holes in his head. But he wanted more, and, soon enough, he found it. Oxycodone.

"Jackpot, mate."

He grabbed every bottle available and deposited them into his pockets, saving one for the present. He unscrewed the lid, dropped two pills into his palm, and dry swallowed them. He was ready to move on when he noticed something else in the cart. He pulled out what looked like a medical swab and read the label.

"Fentynl." He recalled that drug was sometimes mixed with heroin. He removed the paper packaging and saw it was a lozenge on a stick. "Looks like a lolli..."

Saw inserted it into his mouth and sucked on it. It tasted sweet as candy, and within a few moments, he felt some of the pain fade. He grabbed a few more, then decided it best to be on his way.

He followed the red arrows painted on the walls, above which "Exit" was stenciled, and, soon enough, he spied daylight ahead. Before he reached the doorway, he heard a crash inside a nearby room. He approached, cautious, and found an employee's lounge filled with couches, chairs, and vending machines. It was at the snack machine where he saw the zombie.

It knelt on the floor in front of the unit like a man praying to a false idol. When Solomon stepped into the room, it heard him and turned in his direction, revealing other zombies had eaten it to the bone in many places. No skin remained on its head. All of its ribs were visible and its belly was just a hollow cavern. Then Solomon realized why it wasn't coming for him. It was trapped.

The zombie had its right arm inserted all the way into the snack return. A small bag of Cool Ranch Doritos hung precariously, a few inches out of reach. The creature attempted to move toward Saw but made no progress. Its skeletal jaws clicked together like the wind-up teeth they sell in novelty stores. Solomon grinned at the sight.

"Talk about getting your hand caught in the cookie jar. Bad day to be you, mate."

Solomon strode toward the half-eaten zombie, raised the ax overhead, and brought it down in a swift motion that separated the monster's head from his neck. The skull rolled across the floor before getting lost under a jumble of chairs. The body sagged to the ground, except for the arm, which remained trapped inside the machine.

Satisfied, Solomon left the room, then exited the hospital. Several zombies roamed the streets, but he saw no one who was actually alive. He slithered along the sidewalk, keeping close to the buildings and careful to not catch the attention of the undead. He needed a car. A car could take him to his shop, and there he could get prepared. Prepared for the fight he knew was coming.

CHAPTER SEVEN

After three solid days of killing zombies, some of the fun had started to wear off. Meade had lost count at fifty-seven. He'd come upon a scattered group of the monsters outside a K-Mart and dispatched them with his hockey stick. In the melee, he couldn't remember whether there were fourteen or fifteen. That was day two, and he didn't bother keeping track afterward.

His mind was a fog where everything seemed to move in fast forward and slow motion at the same time. Existing on nothing but pre-packaged convenience store junk food wasn't helping.

Mead had raided a Sheetz and filled the trunk of his Cavalier with chips, powdered mini donuts, candy bars, and caffeine-loaded liquids. He felt high, even more than the few times he'd tried cocaine years earlier, but the crash was terrible.

To stave it off, he chugged even more energy drinks (the berry-flavored five-hour energy shots were his favorite) and went back to work. His heart felt as if it might beat out of his chest, but the diet also gave him insatiable fortitude for slicing and dicing the undead bastards.

Even through the excitement and rush, he knew the battle was one he couldn't win. For every zombie he killed, three more showed up. Unless he stumbled upon a tank or an A-bomb, he had no chance of killing all of them.

As he strolled back to his car, he heard a metallic thud in an alleyway to his right. His sugar high was fading, and he almost ignored it. Instead, he wiped remnants of some intestines off his hockey stick and moved between the buildings.

Mead made it five yards into the alley when a small man skittered out from between a row of trash cans. Mead reared back with the stick but stopped when he saw the man hunker down and hold his hands over his head.

"No hurt! No hurt!" the man shouted.

Mead lowered the stick. "What the hell are you doing in the garbage? Do you think you're Oscar the grouch?"

The man peeked up, tentative, but remained silent.

"Stand up."

The man stood, keeping his hands skyward.

"Put your hands down. I'm not gonna hurt you."

He was barely five feet tall and so thin that Mead could see his bones under his parchment paper-colored skin. He reminded Mead of a much older, thinner version of Pan, the busboy whose ear he'd seen eaten away a few days ago.

"Thanks you."

"Yeah," Mead said. "You're welcome. Better watch your back out here."

Mead spun and exited the alley. As he reached for the door handle, he heard the footsteps behind him. He looked back and saw the Asian man waiting a few feet away.

"What?" Mead asked.

"Me go you."

"What?"

"Me go you." The man lifted his hand and mimed holding a steering wheel.

"You want me to take you?"

The man nodded.

"Why?"

The man paused and considered that. Then he shrugged his shoulders. He didn't have an answer. Mead looked from him to the car and tilted his head toward it.

"Well, get in."

The man clapped his hands together three times in rapid succession, then skipped to the Cavalier. He climbed in without giving Mead a chance to change his mind. Mead noticed a few zombies had been drawn to the scene, but they were far enough away to not be a bother. He took a seat behind the wheel, started the engine, then looked over at the little man beside him.

"What's your name?"

"Wang Jie."

Mead grinned. "Wang? Like..." He grabbed his crotch.

Wang nodded. "Wang Jie."

"I can't, man. I just can't." Mead shifted the car into first and eased down the street.

A slow-moving zombie in a paramedic's uniform stumbled toward them, dragging its right leg, which was doused with dried blood. Mead aimed the Cavalier in the zombie's general direction and, when he got up beside it, swung the bladed end of one of his homemade hockey stick weapons and sliced the monster's head clean off.

Mead tossed the stick into the back seat and glanced at his passenger.

"I'm calling you Jie."

They spent the afternoon driving around Johnstown and killing zombies. Around the time it got dark, Mead told Wang Jie they should find a place to sleep. He had no desire to drive all night long, especially with no streetlights to illuminate the way.

As they passed a squat, vinyl-sided building with a sign out front reading, "Pit Stop Beverages," Wang Jie pointed and gesticulated so frantically that Mead thought the old dude might be stroking out.

"Stop here. Stop here!"

"Here?"

Wang Jie nodded, and Mead eased the Cavalier into the empty lot. He parked in front of a hand-painted sign reading "Beer Is Good!" and as soon as the car stopped, the man exited stage right and bounced toward the door.

Mead watched as he pulled a set of keys from his pocket, inserted one into the lock, and swung the steel door open. Then, Wang Jie looked back to Mead and waved for him to come as he disappeared inside.

"I'll be damned," Mead said and followed.

When he got inside, Wang Jie was grabbing liquor bottles off the shelves. The room was on the small side, maybe 20 by 20, but every inch of it was filled with alcohol of various types.

Mead had never been a big drinker but knew how most Americans behaved and was surprised there hadn't been a run on booze in the last days. Or that the store hadn't been looted.

"Take you like," Wang Jie said as he sat his bottles on the counter.

"Is this your store?"

Wang Jie twirled the keys back and forth on his finger. "Wang work here. Two years now. Pay bad. Could no afford good stuff." He unscrewed the top to a bottle of vodka, then took a swig straight from it. Then he tilted the bottle to Mead. "You try."

Mead shook his head. "You go ahead. I'm fine."

Wang shrugged his shoulders and took another long drink. "You loss."

"Is there anything to eat here?"

Wang pointed across the room. "Peanuts. Crackers. That about all."

Mead sighed. "You know what I could really eat? Oranges. Or grapes. Anything but junk food. Hell, I could eat a head of lettuce right about now."

Wang seemed to consider this. "No here. Sorry."

"No worries, buddy."

Two hours later, Wang Jie sang an off-key and mostly incorrect version of "Highway to Hell" while Mead did his best Angus Young impression and played air guitar.

Mead had downed two strawberry-flavored wine coolers and was feeling fine, but he still knew the little Asian man was getting most of the words wrong, and he didn't care. Wang Jie had proved to be quite the lively drunk and hadn't shut his mouth since he'd passed the halfway point on the bottle of Grey Goose.

Eventually, Jie finished his serenade and attempted to take a seat on a folding chair he'd procured from the storage room. He missed and ended up with his ass on the floor.

"Ass hurt!" he said and giggled uncontrollably.

Mead smiled but felt a yawn coming on. He tried to fight it off, but only half succeeded.

"Mead seepy?" Wang asked.

"Very. The last few days have been..."

He didn't finish, and Wang Jie nodded.

"There cot in backroom. You seep there."

"You take the cot, Jie. I can sleep on the floor. After all, this is your place. Kinda."

Wang Jie shook his head almost violently. "You guest. You offend me you no take cot."

"Are you sure?"

"You seep good. Rest well so you drive tomorrow."

Mead did need a good night's sleep. He hadn't had one since this mess started. "Okay, then. You sleep, too, Jie. Maybe I'll let you drive a while tomorrow, too."

Wang Jie giggled again and mimicked holding a steering wheel for the second time in the few hours Mead had known him. He added "Vroom vroom" sounds for effect.

"And maybe not," Mead said, mostly to himself.

He trudged into the backroom, fell onto the cot, and was asleep in seconds.

THE SOUND of smashing glass woke Mead, and the sudden interruption of his sleep left him startled and disoriented. It took him a moment to remember where he was, but once he did, the sounds made a little more sense. Wang Jie must have knocked over a display case. Maybe even an entire row of shelves.

Mead jumped up, worried his new friend might shred himself on broken glass. He rushed to the main room.

Sunlight flooded in through the door, which hung ajar. Mead couldn't believe it was daytime already. He looked around the room but saw no one.

"Jie?"

More glass broke. The sound came from a far corner, an area Mead couldn't see due to the numerous rows of beer and liquor. He started toward the noise, then stopped himself long enough to grab one of his hockey sticks from the counter. Can never be too careful.

He approached. Slow. Cautious. There were eight aisles between him and the wall. Number one was empty. So were two, three, and four. In five, he saw a few cases of beer knocked to the floor. In six, a display rack of various spiced peanuts was toppled over. As he neared row seven, he heard glass crunching underfoot. And then a moan.

Please, let the little bastard be shit-faced, Mead thought. Nothing worse than that.

He liked Jie. Even if they could barely understand each other much of the time, his company was nice. Every time Mead killed a zombie, Wang Jie gave his little clap of approval, and that made Mead feel about as happy as winning a blue ribbon at the county fair.

He stood on the precipice of aisle seven and took a deep breath. After steeling himself, he continued past the shelves toward aisle eight.

Mead didn't find Wang Jie. Instead, he found a middle-aged zombie in a torn housecoat. One of her droopy breasts sagged out from amongst the floral print. Her gray nipple stood erect and swayed back and forth in Mead's direction as if it were shouting, 'Hey there, big fella!'

"What the fuck?"

Mead knew they'd locked the door—locked it and blocked it with a few kegs of beer—to prevent something just like this from happening. But it had happened anyway, and now there was a zombie inside.

Mead strode toward the dead woman, who seemed more interested in reaching for, and knocking down, every bottle of wine on the shelf. As they exploded at her feet, Mead took the knife end of the stick and rammed it through her temple. She fell into the shelf, destroying the remaining bottles of chardonnay.

He pulled his stick free of her skull and again scanned the store. "Jie? Where are you?"

He explored every inch of the building, expecting to find Jie passed out or dead, or undead. His search came up empty. That left only one option. The open door. He noticed the kegs had been pushed to the side but in an orderly manner. This had been done on purpose and gave Mead some hope. The zombie hadn't broken in. Wang Jie had gone out.

Mead stepped into the daylight. The Cavalier sat undisturbed, and he didn't see any zombies in the immediate area. He knew making a spectacle of himself was foolish, but he wanted to find his friend.

"Wang Jie!" he shouted the words, and his call sounded like a thunderclap against the utter silence of the town. "Where the hell did you go?"

He walked up and down the nearest streets, but Jie was nowhere to be found. Mead did see zombies, though, and that reminded him that wandering about was a stupid idea. He returned to the car and recommenced his search on four wheels instead of two feet.

He was passing Ripple Avenue when he spotted a small man at the end of the street. He slammed on the brakes, backed up five feet, and turned up the street. As he did, the man rounded the corner onto Garfield Street. Mead followed.

As the Cavalier breached Garfield, Mead saw the man was only five yards away. He couldn't hold back a relieved smile when he recognized the clothes as Jie's and saw he was carrying a canvas shopping bag.

Mead remembered the man had said something the night before about living a few streets away, and this suddenly made sense. Jie must have gone back to his apartment for something. A dumb, reckless move, but he was alive, and that was what mattered.

Mead pulled up beside Jie and leaned out the window. "I thought you were zombie chow, buddy."

The Cavalier was moving faster than Wang Jie, and Mead moved from seeing his pal from behind to looking him straight in the face. That was when he realized Jie was dead.

The little man's lifeless eyes stared straight ahead. Dried, brown blood covered his left arm, and Mead saw several bite-sized chunks taken out of his bicep area. Mead could see the bone through the wounds.

"You fuckers. There was hardly any meat on him to eat."

He slowed the car, and Wang Jie outpaced him by a few feet. Mead considered driving away, taking the easy way out. But he wouldn't want to go one as one of those revolting, dead fucks and couldn't condemn Jie to that fate, either.

He put the car in park and opened the door. He didn't bother with one of the sticks. Instead, he took a buck knife from his belt as he approached his temporary friend. Mead didn't say anything as he shoved the blade of the knife into the base of Jie's skull. It sank in easily, and when it was buried to the hilt, Mead quickly jerked it from side to side. Jie went limp and collapsed to the ground, and the knife pulled free of his head in the process.

It took him a moment to understand why everything looked so

blurry. He wiped tears from his eyes and snot from his nose, then tried to compose himself.

When he could see clearly, he saw the bag Jie had been carrying. Inside it was an assortment of oranges, apples, and a head of iceberg lettuce which was more brown than green.

"You dumbass. Why'd you go out to get me food? I didn't ask you to do that." His eyes felt like they were on fire and the knife fell from his grip as he brought both of his hands to his face to cover them, to rub them, anything to stop the pain as saltwater poured out, and he sobbed.

He stayed beside Wang Jie's body until he'd composed himself, but even then, his eyes, his whole head, throbbed. He grabbed the knife, then took the bag of food from Jie's dead hand and returned to the Cavalier. It was time to get the hell out of Johnstown once and for all.

CHAPTER EIGHT

After stealing Winebruner's key card and leaving him to die, Mitch continued through the maze until he reached E Wing. There, he found chaos similar to what he'd seen play out in his own bunker. Living people dying, dead people coming back to life, undead people eating the living. Lather, rinse, repeat.

He discovered his mother tucked away in a corner where she huddled over his father. Dear old dad had several ragged bite wounds on his bare shoulders and upper arms. When Mitch looked at him, the only thought that came to mind was, Where's your suit?

His father caught him staring and looked up with fevered, yellow eyes. "Mitchell. You're alive. Thank God."

Mitch's mother turned, and when she saw him, she gave him a crushing embrace like the one he received upon arriving at the Greenbrier. This time, Mitch pulled away immediately. The two of them looked so pathetic as they sulked, helpless and passive on the floor. These were the people who'd kept him under their thumbs his entire life. Now, they looked like cowed dogs.

"It's falling apart," his father hissed, and bloody spittle leaked out from between his colorless lips.

Mitch nodded. "It's over. Your money. Your power. Those things you spent your life chasing, they're all worthless now. Now, all that matters is how fast you can run."

He saw sheer terror in his father's eyes, a look Mitch found both unnerving and satisfying at the same time. Everyone gets theirs in the end, he thought.

Just then, Mitch spotted a drop-dead gorgeous woman. He immediately recognized her as the wife of Senator Fitzpatrick from NY.

Normally, Mitch couldn't be bothered to give a shit about his father's colleagues or their spouses, but this woman stuck in his mind because she was a Czech fashion model before tying the knot. When her countless nude photos leaked, it became a modest scandal. Now, Magda or Marta or whatever her name was, dashed around the bunker in a silk nightgown that did little to conceal her ample tits or perfectly round ass.

As Mitch admired the woman, a zombie dove at her and bit a mouthful of flesh out of a juicy butt cheek. What a waste. It made him think of Rochelle, and he wondered if she'd become zombie chow as well. That, too, would be a waste.

The woman screamed and struggled, and her tits popped free, but zombies descended upon her and tore away her flesh in heaping mouthfuls. That ruined Mitch's cheap thrill.

He pulled his mother close to him. Her confused gaze drifted around the room, taking in random bits of chaos. Mitch pitied her, but that pity turned to annoyance when she refused to meet his gaze. He grabbed her chin and forced her to make eye contact with him.

"He's going to die. Not just die but turn into one of them." Mitch cocked a thumb toward the zombies roaming about, eating people.

Tears burst from Margaret's eyes. "No. That won't happen. Not to your father. It can't."

Mitch shook her, hard. Even though she was taller, he was stronger, and she snapped out of her hysterics. "Are you going to die with him, or are you going to try to live?"

She looked back to her husband, who picked at one of the larger wounds with his fingertips. He peeled back a thick strip of flesh and stared at it, curious.

"I... We can't leave him, Mitch. What would people think?"

It took every bit of restraint Mitch had to resist slapping her hard across the face. He almost did anyway, just to see how it would feel. He stopped himself, though, because the scales were tipping fast inside E Wing. The zombies nearly outnumbered the people, and he didn't want to call any attention to them. To himself.

"Decide now, Mother. We're almost out of time."

She looked to her husband, to the chaos overrunning the room, and then back to Mitch. Margaret grabbed his hand. "Go."

They took off in a quick jog as Mitch led her away from the carnage.

His father didn't protest; he was too busy digging his fingers into his own arm, at least he did until the Speaker of the House dove on top of him and gnawed away at the soft, exposed flesh on his belly. Senator SOB died with his eyes open as he watched his own shit-filled intestines being devoured.

CHAPTER NINE

WIM SAT IN THE BRONCO AND WATCHED THE MAN FOR ALMOST thirty minutes, and he still wasn't sure if he was alive, dead, or undead. The man was old and black. He sat still as a statue on a park bench overlooking the river. Wim eventually decided that sitting and staring wasn't doing either of them any good, so he grabbed one of his pistols and exited the truck.

When he was ten feet away, the man turned and glanced in his direction. His movements were slow and stiff. For a moment, Wim thought he was a zombie after all.

When he saw the man's face, he saw life. He noticed the man's cheeks were shiny and tear-streaked and regretted bringing the gun. Wim tried to hide it in his pocket, but the grip still poked out notoriously.

"Are you friend or foe?" Emory asked as he wiped the wetness from his cheeks with the back of a gnarled, arthritis-swollen hand.

"A friend, I promise."

"And I accept your promise. I, myself, am unarmed. And a friend would be most welcome."

They sat in the shade cast by a grove of silver maples, which had recently broken out in foliage. There, they shared their stories of how they had survived the outbreak and subsequent chaos. Wim didn't go into great detail over exterminating his hometown, but he did tell Emory about the mailman and his chance encounter with Ramey.

Emory broke down when he spoke of Christopher and again as he described the fraternity brothers who had saved his life. Wim thought him somewhat weepy in general, but the old man's kindness was clear. Emory was a good four inches taller than Wim but skinny as a rail. He reminded Wim of his father in that regard. His short hair had gone snow white but hadn't receded, and he seemed sharp as a tack mentally.

They shared a can of ravioli Emory had scavenged, eating it with their bare hands.

"Grant would be absolutely distraught to see me right now," Emory said and chuckled. He popped another bite into his mouth. "Eating like a toddler."

"I suspect we'll be eating out of a lot of cans from here on out."

"Why is that?"

"I haven't seen any animals since the flu took out my stock. Not even a crow flying overhead or a squirrel running across the road."

Emory's peaceful expression faded as he considered that. "Now that you mention it, neither have I."

"Our country took food for granted. Took a lot of things for granted. But if all the animals died, that means no fresh meat, no dairy products. And I reckon no one's going to plant and harvest fields for a while. All that leaves is packaged food."

"So, why did you leave your farm? I hope you don't find that question improper; I'm genuinely curious."

Wim looked to the river, where the clean, clear waters trickled along lazily, and ran his hand through his shoe polish black hair. "My pa was German, but I guess my surname tipped you to that. He was born there and came over as a teenager.

"He didn't speak much Dutch, but he had a couple sayings. One of them was, 'Einer all in ist nict enmal im paradise,' or something along those lines. He said it meant being alone is not good, even in paradise. I've been alone a long time, and it never bothered me much. But now that almost everything else is gone, well, I suppose I thought it was time to quit taking other people for granted because you never know when they'll be gone for good."

"That's quite wise, my new, young friend."

Wim felt his cheeks get hot. "That might have been the most words I've ever said all at one time."

Emory gave him a pat on the thigh. "You've been saving them up."

"Maybe."

"Do you have a particular itinerary or destination in mind?"

"The girl I mentioned, she was going to West Virginia to look for her father."

Wim glanced at Emory to see what reaction that stirred. Emory gave a warm, comforting smile. "And you hope to stumble upon her trail?"

Wim shrugged. He checked the can and saw Chef Boyardee's kitchen was closed. He stood and carried the can to a wastebasket, then dropped it in. When he turned back to Emory, the man had also risen and was stretching out a body full of aches.

"I'd like to join you, if you're amenable to some company."

"Company would be nice."

"Good. I have a few more cans of food and some soda pop in the van. Let me gather that together. The least this old hitchhiker can do is supply some nourishment."

As they progressed deeper into West Virginia, the roads became narrower and the population even more sparse. That was a turn for the positive as it meant fewer zombies, and the few they did spot, they didn't bother killing.

While Emory napped on and off, Wim had driven a few hundred miles. The setting sun fell below the mountains and plunged the valley they were traveling through into darkness. As they rounded a sharp curve, the headlights of the Bronco didn't illuminate the horde of zombies until it crashed into them at thirty miles an hour.

CHAPTER TEN

THE NEED TO EVACUATE HIS BOWELS HAD BEEN BUILDING FOR half an hour. Bundy knew he should pull the van to the side of the road, drop trou, and do his business, but after months in prison where he had to shit on open-air toilets where anyone could and did walk by whenever they wanted, he had grown to appreciate bathrooms with doors.

Every rumble in his belly was louder and more dangerous than the last, so when he saw the sign reading, "Rest Stop - 2 mi," he breathed a heavy sigh of relief.

The parking lot was empty save for an old Chevy pickup towing a pop-up Coleman camper. As he parked as close as he could get to the plain, concrete building, he saw no one. He switched off the engine and climbed free of the van, then duck-walked toward the entrance, clenching his ample ass cheeks together at the same time.

He shoved the steel entry door open, slamming it against the wall. Inside, the men's room appeared empty. The gross, sweet smell of urinal cakes burned his nose, but he ignored it as he scurried to the nearest stall.

It was a regular unit, and he barely fit through the doorway. The handicap john at the other end of the room would have been more comfortable, but the rumbles in his belly had turned to quakes that could be measured on the Richter scale, and he wasn't about to push his luck.

Bundy unbuckled his belt, pushed down his pants and underwear, and felt the shit start gushing out of his asshole like hot pudding as he was still dropping onto the seat. Fortunately, he had solid aim and breathed a sigh of relief as he heard his droppings plunge into the toilet water.

"Bullseye," he said with a contented smile. He sat there for several minutes as the raging river slowed to a trickle. He suspected round two might be coming, so he waited.

A few minutes later, and around the time he thought he might be finished defecating, he heard the restroom door open.

I just wanted to shit in peace, he thought. He considered calling out, "Occupied," but decided to wait in silence.

Footsteps of the slow, dragging variety moved into the room, and with every step, they grew closer to Bundy's stall. He realized he was holding his breath and exhaled slowly, soundlessly.

Whatever, or whoever it was, crept toward Bundy's stall, stopped in front, and stood there. Bundy attempted to peer under the small gap at the bottom of the door, but he was squeezed into the small stall and had no room to maneuver.

Ten seconds passed. Twenty. Then the footsteps moved on. They continued to the end of the row of stalls, then returned. They paused again at Bundy's stall. He heard a noise. Sniffling? No, sniffing. Well, that's pretty disgusting, he thought. The sniffer took a few more whiffs, then vacated the room.

Bundy waited long enough to deem the coast clear, wiped several times, and tried to flush. The toilet gave a weak gurgle but did nothing to make the mess he'd left behind vanish. He closed the lid and hoped the next person to come along didn't have the misfortune of checking stall number one.

He opened the stall door and double-checked to make sure the room was empty. After verifying it was, he continued to the exit. The space outside the men's room also appeared vacant. He was unsure to where the sniffer had disappeared, but he was fine with letting the mystery of the bathroom interloper remain unsolved. Let the Hardy Boys tackle that caper.

Bundy made it halfway to the van when he heard the voice.

"Mister?"

The voice was weak and inconsequential and almost got lost in the wind.

"Hey, Mister?"

Bundy turned and scanned the area. Soon enough, he saw someone. He thought it was a boy, but it could have been a girl with short hair. He'd rarely been around children and guessed this one to be five or six years old.

He noticed the child wore a medical boot on its left leg, and the dragging footsteps made more sense.

"Mister, my daddy's stuck."

"Stuck?"

"I can't get him out. I'm not big enough. Come help him!"

With that, the kid took off in an awkward, loping run. It disappeared around the block building. Bundy, refreshed after his recent bathroom adventures, followed.

The boy, and it was a boy he realized when he saw him closer up—stood in front of what looked like a hole in the ground. When Bundy reached the scene, he saw it was a hole of sorts but a man-made one of the concrete variety.

It was a small chute, about seven feet deep. At the bottom was a doorway one-third the normal size, and Bundy assumed it was an access door to a crawlspace or service area.

Also occupying the small space was a man slumped against the wall. Bundy could only see the top of his head, which revealed a half-bald pate that had sustained several cuts and gashes. The man sat motionless.

"Daddy! I brought help!" The boy peered into the pit, eagerly waiting for his father's reaction. Bundy did the same, and, soon enough, the trapped man moved.

First, he slumped forward, putting his hands on the ground and crawling onto all fours like a dog. Then, he pushed himself upward, where he swayed precariously on his feet.

"Help him out, Mister. Please, help my daddy."

Bundy glanced at the kid and saw his rust-colored hair flip up as a gust of wind caught it, then settle back down when it passed. A constellation of freckles spread across his cheeks and nose, and Bundy thought he looked a bit like he'd always imagined Huckleberry Finn.

"Come on, Mister."

Bundy leaned over the hole. The man rocked back and forth on his feet. He still hadn't looked up.

"Hey, buddy. Hell of a spot you got yourself in down there."

The man groaned in response.

"He hurt himself when he fell," the boy said.

Bundy glanced at the boy and felt sick when he saw the eagerness plastered on his face. "He did, huh?"

The boy nodded. "That's why you've gotta help him."

Bundy turned back to the man. He'd stopped his marching in place and now looked upward, toward their voices. The right side of the man's face was smashed in like a partially crushed can of soda. His mouth hung ajar, allowing pink drool to dribble out. And when he saw the two humans above him, he unleashed another groan.

"What are you waiting for? Help him!"

The boy gave Bundy a shove in the ribs. Bundy sat on his rump and stared the boy in the eyes.

"Listen, buddy. Your dad's not hurt."

"Yes, he is!"

"No, he might have been hurt before. But he's more than hurt now. He's dead."

"No, he ain't. He's moving. Dead people don't move."

He had a point there, and Bundy wasn't exactly sure how to

respond. Instead, he stood up and grabbed the kid's tiny hand, which was swallowed up in his catcher's mitt of a paw.

"You have to listen to me. He's dead. There was a sickness. It made people die but left 'em able to move around. All clumsy-like." God, that sounded ridiculous. No wonder the kid wasn't buying it.

"You're crazy! You're a crazy man! Let me go!"

Jesus, why did I pick this place to shit, Bundy thought. "Come with me. I'll show you that there are others like him. There's no saving them."

Bundy walked and pulled the kid along. He squirmed and struggled, but he was little more than a rag doll compared to the big man. They made it all the way to the van, and Bundy slid open the rear door. He turned to the kid, ready to lift him into the ride, when the boy uncorked a perfectly aimed punch to his nuts.

The breath rushed out of him in a pained, "Oooooof," and he grabbed his balls with both hands. With that, the kid bolted toward the rest stop. Toward his dead father.

"Wait, kid!" Bundy trudged after him, but between his mammoth size and the throbbing agony between his legs, he was very slow going. "Stay away from your dad! He's a zombie!" When Bundy rounded the corner, the boy was nowhere to be seen. "Kid? Hey? Where are you?"

Bundy continued on, toward the pit at the side of the building. When he reached it, he paused.

"Don't do this. Not this time." He took a deep breath and looked into the pit.

The first thing he saw was the boy's bright blue medical boot. Then he saw the rest of the boy sprawled across his father's lap. It appeared as if he was cradling his son. Maybe rocking him to sleep or singing him a lullaby like he'd done before the world turned to shit. It could have been saccharine sweet.

But it wasn't. Because the father wasn't holding his son. He was eating him.

When the father looked up at Bundy, his cheeks bulged out like a chipmunk that had been gathering acorns for winter. A stringy strip of flesh hung out from between his teeth, and his jaws chomped up and down, up and down until it disappeared into his mouth.

"You prick."

The zombie dad growled at him, then leaned in to the kid and bit off his bottom lip. Bundy had seen enough. He headed back to the van and tried to put what he saw out of his mind.

CHAPTER ELEVEN

The tide had swamped the Saab on the beach, but Bolivar didn't care. The three-mile walk in the cool, damp ocean breeze gave him time to clear his head. When he arrived at the village of Lewes and found it overrun with zombies—just like Philadelphia but on a smaller scale—any optimism he'd built up on his morning stroll vanished.

It really is over, he thought. His medic training hadn't included courses on virology, but he knew anything which could spread that fast was beyond control. The world as he'd known it was gone. Accepting that proved freeing in some regards.

He gave little thought to trekking to Illinois to track down his father and brother or to California, where his sister had moved the week after she graduated high school. He hoped they had survived but trying to reconnect was pointless. That life was over.

He suspected the government was over, too, but he decided that as soon as he secured a vehicle, he'd take Sawyer's advice and continue to Dover Air Force Base, mostly because he didn't know where else to go.

He'd enlisted in the Army when he was still a junior in high school. His father had fought in the first Iraq war, and Bolivar, who was a mediocre student with little athletic prowess, was expected to follow in his footsteps and become a soldier.

The problem was that he couldn't fathom killing people. He appreciated the structure of the military, the camaraderie, and especially the unknown—in the U.S. one day and halfway around the globe the next—but he thought himself incapable of shooting another human being.

One of his instructors in boot camp, a bespectacled Yankee with a thick Maine accent, picked up on Bolivar's hesitance during firearms training drills. One day, he pulled him aside and confronted him.

"You got good eyes on you, but every time you pull the trigga, you close 'em."

Bolivar hemmed and hawed and tried to say he didn't have experience with firearms. That part was true, but the Yankee saw through it.

"Not everyone's meant to be down in the dirt fightin and scrapin and killin. Some folks got to hang back a bit and clean up the mess. I reckon that might suit you betta."

He was the one who told Bolivar to consider becoming a combat medic, and as soon as the words were out of his pinched mouth, Bolivar knew it was his future. He finished basic, then was shipped off to Fort Sam Houston in Texas, where he spent over a year learning the skills of the job.

He'd found his calling, and in more than a decade of service, he'd managed to not kill anyone. The zombie he shot through the windshield of the smart car was the only thing he'd ever shot, and he hardly thought that counted.

Lewes was a small town with a canal running through the middle of it. As he approached the village, a squat lighthouse greeted him. Painted on the side was "Welcome to Historic Lewes, Delaware. The first town in the first state," and below the writing, an old pickup had smashed through the fake, brown lighthouse. Bolivar checked the ignition, but the keys were gone.

The zombies grew thicker the further he got into town, and dozens of them filled the once quaint main streets. The buildings were vintage and brick and had carefully painted wood accents. It was the type of place you'd see on a postcard saying, "Wish you were here." *Wish I wasn't.*

He came upon a Chevy Cruze and a Ford Escape that had tapped together in a minor fender bender and were now abandoned. The Escape was keyless, but he had better luck with the Cruze. Bolivar turned the key, and the car started. He'd avoided the zombies until that point, but the sound of the engine drew their attention.

As he backed away from the Ford and made a U-turn in the middle of the street, a few dozen of them came running after him. Another five approached from the front. Bolivar saw one of them was a young girl with yellow hair, which reminded him of the drawings he'd found in the Saab's trunk.

This girl was dead, and when he drove toward her, she jumped onto the hood and snarled at him through the windshield. Bolivar gunned the engine, and the Chevy jumped forward, smashing into two grown-up zombies who happened to be in his path.

They toppled in opposite directions, and the girl lost her grip, rolling sideways off the hood. Bol glanced in the rearview mirror as he drove away and saw all three of them back on their feet and stumbling after him, no worse for the wear.

He took Highway 1 North toward Dover and made good time because there wasn't a single other moving vehicle on the entire forty-mile drive. He saw a few abandoned cars and several of the crashed variety, but he had the road to himself aside from a few zombies that wandered around, appearing lost and alone.

Dover Air Force Base was off Exit 35, and Bolivar steered the Cruze down the ramp. When he turned right at the light, the sign out front signaled he had arrived. No soldiers manned the gates, which stood wide open.

A dirty, camo-colored Humvee blocked the road, and on it, someone had spray painted, "This is the END. Repent!" Inside the vehicle, a zombie soldier saw Bolivar and desperately clawed at the window. His fingers left red streaks against the glass. Behind the gates, a handful of dead soldiers were scattered about like roadkill.

Bolivar didn't bother to check the base. It was obvious that there was nothing left to find. He threw the car into reverse and spun the car a hundred eighty degrees. As he faced back at the highway, he looked down the barrel of an AK-47.

CHAPTER TWELVE

Someone had been following Aben for the last couple of days. He'd never seen them but heard enough branches breaking and leaves rustling to play Sherlock Holmes and deduce the obvious. It wasn't a zombie, that much was certain. Those clumsy oafs could barely walk a straight line down the highway, let alone partake in a rousing game of cat and mouse, so that meant it had to be someone else who had survived the plague.

Aben hadn't seen a single living person since escaping jail. The idea that someone else was out there and close by gave him more anxiety than comfort, especially if it was the type of person who preferred to stay unseen.

He'd walked about forty miles since leaving the town, sticking mostly to the highways, which were refreshingly free of zombies. He passed dozens of abandoned cars with keys still in the ignition but hadn't bothered jacking a ride. He had nowhere to go and wasn't in a hurry to get there.

Instead, he raided the vehicles for food and supplies. He lucked into four pistols. Gotta love rural America, he thought and added them to his rucksack. He still kept Dolan's gun tucked into his belt, and beside it was the hammer sledge.

Aben had used the sledge seventeen times so far, and it had proved its value over and over again. It was heavy and awkward, but one good blow to the head dropped the zombies each and every time. It didn't matter if he hit them in the top, front, back, or sides of their skulls. The hammer produced a satisfying crunch and a dead, or deader, zombie. He hadn't needed the guns at all.

The western sky was a watercolor painting of pink and purple clouds, and the light had faded to the point where he couldn't see fifty feet ahead. When he came to a rusty Jeep Cherokee, he decided to make it camp for the night.

The truck, like most of the vehicles he came across, had its fair share of trash inside, and Aben constructed a rough circle of garbage around it. His sleep had been restless, and he was certain to hear anything that stepped on the litter during the night.

Aben sat behind the wheel of the Jeep and ate half a can of beans (maple cured bacon flavor) and an entire bag of barbecue chips. He was uncomfortable being in the driver's seat, even in a vehicle that wasn't moving. He hadn't driven a vehicle in over twenty-five years, not since the war.

The last time he'd driven, he steered a Humvee carrying himself and four of his fellow marines into an IED. Aben survived with a windshield worth of glass to the face, two ruptured eardrums, and a concussion that had him seeing stars and hearing bells for months. Three of the others didn't survive, so, all things considered, he was lucky.

He was lucky now, too, and he was thinking about how many times he'd escaped death when he dozed off. It was full dark when the scratching of a soda can against the pavement roused him. He came awake quickly but couldn't see anything in the black void of night. A flick of the headlight lever illuminated the road ahead, and that's when he saw it run.

The dog was medium-sized and either muddy brown or dirty

yellow in color. It was skinny and its ribs stood out against its short-haired coat. He only saw its ass end and couldn't guess at the breed as it dashed away from the light and into the trees that guarded the highway like rows of infantry.

Something else had survived, he thought. The dog was the first living creature he'd seen since this mess began. He eased open the Jeep door and dropped down from the vehicle.

He gave a low whistle and waited. He heard nothing. Probably gone for good. Nonetheless, he took the remnants of the beans and knocked them onto the roadway a few yards ahead of the Jeep, then he crawled back inside and eventually drifted back to sleep.

Just before dawn, he woke again. The beans were gone, and so was the dog. Aben repacked his bag and hit the road. Around noon, he stopped to rest by a Tastycake Delivery truck that had rolled down the embankment and onto its side.

He gorged on banana pudding cupcakes and powdered mini donuts until his stomach bulged and made him look a few months pregnant. He saw movement in his peripheral vision and reached for the hammer, but as his eyes focused, he saw the dog.

It was twenty yards away, but he could see it better in the daylight. It looked like a yellow lab but smaller in stature and with big, triangle ears that stood straight up. A mutt for sure. He saw the dog had a dark brown spot on its left hindquarter that looked like dried blood.

Aben grabbed a vanilla cupcake, removed it from the wrapper, and chucked it at the dog like he was lobbing a grenade.

The dog hopped up and backed away. When it did, Aben could see it was limping. The cupcake bounced and rolled along the grass. The dog looked at it, then to Aben, then back to the food. It approached it, cautious, taking two steps back for every three forward, but it got there eventually.

The dog sniffed the cupcake, then gave it an exploratory lick. It looked again to Aben before snatching the food up in its jaws and running for cover in the forest.

That's okay, Aben thought. There's no hurry.

HE STAYED on the highway and had reached a blink-and-you-miss-it town in Maryland when he came upon the most zombies he'd found clustered together since escaping the prison. He knew the hammer alone wouldn't be sufficient. He wasn't fond of guns. They were loud and made a spectacle, but sometimes they were necessary. Like now.

Aiming the pistol with one hand was a challenge, and his first shot went high. As the roar of the report echoed through the valley, the zombies turned in his direction and came for him.

The next four rounds connected. Good, clean headshots. A few of the zombies further back in the pack stumbled over their fallen comrades, and he quickly put three more down.

Dolan's pistol was empty, so Aben dropped it and dug through the sack for another. The first he found was a cheap Hi-Point 9mm. Earlier, he'd chambered a round, a task which had taken several minutes and the use of his feet, but now he was glad he'd made the effort.

He shot the closest zombie and went to fire again, but the gun jammed.

"Son of a bitch!" he muttered and dropped the pistol. He reached for another, but the zombies were within ten feet of him and closing in quickly. He grabbed the hammer instead and marched toward them.

A raven-haired boy in a Little League uniform was the first to fall under the maul. Then Aben dropped an elderly woman wearing nothing but a pale, blue housecoat. Next was a middle-aged man in coke-bottle glasses, and Aben smashed the hammer into the bridge of his nose. His face crumpled inward, and it fell in a heap at Aben's feet.

Three zombies remained, and they'd surrounded him. A zombie in bib overalls and a teen in a Maroon 5 tee shirt were at his right, and a woman in a UPS uniform was to his left. He hit the farmer first and raised the hammer again to take out the Adam Levin fanboy. As he reared back, the delivery girl grabbed his arm. He shook free and gave a glancing blow to the teen but only caught it in the jaw.

Bits of teeth fell from its mouth and clattered against the street like tic tacs. Its jaw hung open and crooked, and it groaned but kept coming at him.

The UPS driver grabbed him again, and Aben could feel its moist breath against the back of his neck. Its wet growls were so close. Close enough to bite.

He swung his left elbow back and connected with the woman's chest, which pushed her back a step, but she didn't let go. The toothless zombie in front pushed against him. It was a full foot shorter than Aben, and its face was only inches from his chest. It pressed its broken mouth against Aben's beard, but its destroyed jaw kept it from biting.

Thank God for small favors.

The zombie at his back closed in again, and the guttural sounds of her growls filled his ears. He dropped the hammer and reached back with his right hand, his remaining hand, and grabbed a fistful of her curly brunette hair. She growled again, louder, closer.

He tried to hold her off while the teen in front of him crowded in and pushed against him and grabbed him by the shoulders. They both reeked of death. Not to the extent of Dolan's rotting body in that hot, small room, but like three-day-old road kill. The up close and personal assault on his nostrils made a bad situation even worse. Aben was the meat in a zombie bread sandwich.

If only I had two hands, he thought. I could get out of this if I still had two damned hands.

But he didn't. His stump had stopped oozing and copious amounts of ibuprofen held the pain at bay, but his left arm was little more than a club, especially in situations like this, when it mattered. Nearly two decades in the Marines and another twenty-plus years hitching around the country at the mercy of truckers and potential serial killers, and here he was, ready to get taken out by a brown Santa and a pop music groupie. It was almost funny.

The tension in his arm from holding her hair suddenly vanished, and Aben's hand came free with a clump of her brunette curls and a hunk of skin from her scalp. She dove onto him, and he fell back against the teen.

The three of them went down in a pile of flailing limbs. The UPS driver's face was against his own cheek when a blur of yellow flew by Aben's eyes, and the female zombie toppled off him.

Aben heard the snarling and gasping and rolled free of the pile. He found the hammer sledge under the Maroon 5 fan and yanked it free. The boy tried to get up, but before he could, Aben brought the angled end of the hammer down on his head. It sunk into the skull and the resulting sound reminded Aben of cracking a hard-boiled egg. It felt good.

He spun sideways and scrambled to his knees with the hammer ready to strike whatever was within reach. That was when he saw the dog. The mongrel tore at the throat of the UPS zombie, which swung its arms, trying to get free. Aben watched for a moment. Long tendrils of shredded flesh stretched from the zombie's mangled throat to the dog's snarling jaws.

When the zombie grabbed onto the dog's floppy ear, it yelped in pain, and Aben quickly raised the hammer and smashed it into the dead woman's forehead. Her previously pretty face collapsed inward in a black pit of coagulated blood, bone, and cartilage. The monster stopped moving, and the dog released the torn, rotting skin.

Aben reached for the animal, moving too fast despite knowing better, and the dog bolted away from him. It ran ten yards before pausing and looking back.

"You're okay. I won't hurt you. I promise."

It hunkered coiled like a spring, every muscle in its body tensed and ready to flee.

Aben backed away slowly, retreating to his bag. He ruffled through the contents and came out with half a package of beef jerky.

He threw one piece to the dog and watched as it first jumped back, then inched forward and took it in its mouth.

The dog chewed it up in three quick bites, then looked up to Aben. He thought it looked wary and expectant at the same time. He threw another piece but made sure that one landed a few yards short. The dog belly crawled to it, then ate it.

They repeated that toss and eat game four more rounds, and the dog was soon within five feet. That time, Aben didn't throw the jerky. Instead, he held it in his extended palm and waited for the dog to come to him.

After about a minute, it did just that. It backed away after taking it, out of reach, but didn't run. After it swallowed, Aben set the last piece on the ground at his feet.

"You don't have to be scared of me. Come on and get it."

The dog did, and when it finished eating, it sat at Aben's feet and looked up at his bearded and scarred face. Its tail flopped back and forth, thudding against the pavement, and Aben smiled.

He extended his arm and scratched the dog behind the ear. He could feel its fur was dirty and matted. The pungent odor wasn't as bad as the zombies, but it was close. That was okay. Aben knew he didn't smell like rosewater either. The more he scratched, the faster the dog's tail wagged.

He saw the brown spot on the dog's hindquarter was dried blood. When he pushed apart the fur to get a better look, the dog tensed but didn't run. Aben found a wound the size of a half dollar which was bright red and festering pus. A handful of maggots writhed in the gash. Again with the maggots, he thought. If he never saw maggots again as long as he lived, it would be too soon.

"You'll be okay. You saved me. Now, I'll return the favor."

The dog crawled onto his lap and licked his face. It felt good to not be alone.

CHAPTER THIRTEEN

JULI THOUGHT WHAT HAD HAPPENED IN HER PICTURE-PERFECT suburban home was Hell, but that opinion changed when she reached the city. She'd planned to go to the police station and turn herself in. What exactly she would say was still something of a mystery, even though she'd been rehearsing it as she drove.

"Well, you see, officer, my husband murdered our daughter. Then he tried to murder me, but I killed him first. Then I went to check on my son, and he was a zombie. No, officer, I'm not psychotic. No, I'm not taking hallucinogens. That's really what happened."

No one would believe that, of course. Juli herself barely believed it, and she lived through it. Maybe she had lost her mind. In some ways, that might be for the best because she didn't know how she could live through what happened.

The night sky brightened as she neared the city, but it wasn't just the sea of streetlights that lit up the skyline as usual. Orange, shimmery smoke danced through the air like Baryshnikov, and the closer she came to the city, the brighter the night grew.

Even for a city, the streets seemed unusually occupied considering the time of night. People dashed aimlessly in every direction, carrying everything from TVs and stereos to toilet paper and jugs of water.

I'm driving straight into a riot, Juli thought. That there might be a correlation between the carnage in her home and the chaos in the city didn't even cross her mind.

A small teenage Asian boy ran past the front of her SUV, and if she'd been going five MPH faster, she'd have hit him. She slammed on her brakes, and he glanced back over his shoulder and mimed slitting his throat.

"Watch where you going, whore!"

You little punk, she thought but didn't say it, not even from behind the safety of her locked doors and windows. The teen ran off, and she kept driving.

She saw a few people staggering about in a manner that reminded her of Mark but tried to ignore them. *That's not possible. They're old or hurt. That's all.*

The smoke grew thicker as she closed in on a block of Government housing units. She saw smoke leaking from the windows on the upper floors, but there weren't any fire trucks on the scene. Instead, there stood a row of military vehicles. A few soldiers brandished big black guns as they stood guard outside the entryways. They stared at Juli as she passed by but didn't move to stop her.

When she reached the next brick complex, she saw more soldiers, only instead of guns, they had tanks strapped to their backs. Juli thought they must be some sort of firefighters. When two black men ran out of the building, she quickly realized the soldiers weren't fighting the fires. They were starting them.

The soldiers spun toward the fleeing black men and aimed their nozzles. What came next was something Juli knew she'd never forget as long as she lived. From the nozzles gushed long sprays of fire, and the fire rained down on the two black men and coated their bodies in flames.

They ran another ten feet, staggered and stumbled for five more, then fell to the ground, arms and legs flailing. Juli could hear their screams, which were high and strangely feminine, even with the windows up. The soldiers turned to her and waved her by. Nothing to see here. She drove on.

A few streets down, she reached a roadblock. A Dodge Charger police cruiser sat upside down on its roof. The siren blared. Dozens of people rocked it back and forth. Some had climbed onto the upside-down undercarriage and jumped up and down, gleeful. Juli watched as several men dragged two police officers through the car's shattered windshield and into the streets, where the crowd pummeled them.

Juli made a hard right into an alley. As her headlights lit up the narrow tunnel, she saw another police officer kneeling over a homeless man.

When she neared them, she saw the officer's face buried in the man's belly. When the noise of the SUV got the cop's attention, it looked up, and Juli saw blood and flesh dripping from its mouth.

She screamed and hit the gas. The SUV vaulted forward and bounced over the cop's legs. Juli checked the rearview mirror and saw it had returned to eating the bum. She was still looking behind her when she exited the alley, and it was only the chorus of screams that drew her attention forward.

To her left, she saw row after row of police SWAT officers clad head to toe in black uniforms and body armor. Most held Plexiglas shields in front of them. As chunks of bricks, glass bottles, and assorted debris soared through the air, the need for them became clear.

To Juli's right were hundreds of residents of the city. Most were young and black, but several whites, Latinos, and Asians were mixed in. They held weapons of all kinds: guns, rifles, bats, shovels. They shouted at the police, and through the cacophony of voices, Juli heard their demands.

"Let us out! Let us out!"

"We have rights! You can't keep us here!"

"Fuck the pigs!"

Ragged coughs and sneezes rang out from both sides of the impasse.

The crowd of city dwellers moved forward. There were only twenty feet separating them from the police. Juli shut off the lights of the SUV and put it in reverse, letting it drift silently back into the cover of the alleyway. She stayed close enough to watch.

A teen ran to the front of the crowd and launched a forty-ounce beer bottle at the police. It somersaulted through the air and smashed into the face of a beefy cop who had picked the wrong time to look sideways instead of straight ahead. He collapsed as if he'd been shot, and two officers beside him raised their rifles, ready to shoot.

"Hold your fire! That's an order!" a blond-haired cop who tried to keep control screamed into a bullhorn. Then he turned toward the crowd. "There is a curfew in effect! Go back to your homes! You're safe there!"

"The fuck we are! Fucking pigs just want to make it easier to butcher us!" That came from a giant black man with a shaved head and bushy gray beard. He held a shotgun which was leveled at the rows of police. "We ain't stupid!"

The giant cocked the shotgun and held his finger to the trigger.

"Put down the weapon!" the cop in charge shouted.

The stand-off lasted maybe three seconds but felt like a minute. Then the giant fired.

Birdshot slammed into police officers. Most received minor wounds, if injured at all, but one officer caught a BB in the eye and went to his knees, holding his face. Blood seeped out from his fingers.

"Don't shoot! Hold your fire!"

One officer threw a can of tear gas into the rioters. Two more followed. Any chance of the stalemate ending peacefully went up in thick, yellow smoke.

Someone new shot. Juli couldn't tell which group fired first, but it didn't matter because more shots rang out in both directions. Bodies hit the ground on each side. Then the two groups raced toward each other. The battle was on.

Two teens beat a cop to death with baseball bats.

An officer with a rifle fired again and again and again, dropping half a dozen people in mere seconds.

Someone tossed Molotov cocktails, and a trio of cops went up in flames.

A cop shot a boy in the throat. Then, as the boy lay dying in front of him, the cop put his pistol to his own temple and blew off the top half of his head.

After that, Juli saw a rioter, who was sprawled prone on the ground as he was being chomped on by another protestor, jump to its feet and run at the cops. He tackled an officer to the ground, then leaned in and ate away the cop's ear.

"Oh, dear God," Juli said to herself. She couldn't believe it was happening. She wished she'd stayed in her house and died with her family. That would have been better than being out here with these monsters, with nowhere to go. Just waiting to be killed. Out here, she was going to die alone.

The blond cop who'd been in charge tried to fight off another officer who had a knife sticking out of its throat. The blond cop beat it with the bullhorn, but two other zombies joined in. Juli could hear him shrieking as he was eaten alive.

Within minutes, at least half the crowd were members of the undead, and this new faction fought together to destroy the living. Cops attacked fellow cops. Rioters ate other rioters. So much blood flowed that Juli saw it gushing down the gutter and into the sewer grates.

She stared out at the carnage unfolding before her, frozen, until a zombie slammed into the grill of her SUV. It was a female police officer, her ginger ponytail twisted askew under her riot helmet. Her throat was torn out, and Juli could see gristly tendons and veins exposed. The zombie pulled itself up the hood and grabbed onto the windshield wiper. Its face pressed against the glass, smearing red splotches.

"Get off!" Juli yelled. She hit the wipers, which swished to and fro and dragged the zombie's arm back and forth in an undead wave. Juli smacked her hand against the inside of the windshield. "Get off!" she tried again, not sure why she was even saying the pointless, useless words out loud.

The zombie's face was even with hers, and she looked into its dull, gray eyes. There was nothing alive left inside those eyes. It made her think of the eyes of a swordfish Mark had caught on one of their vacations to Key West and later had mounted to hang on the wall of his man cave.

As Juli stared into the dead woman's eyes, the zombie's head bounced off the windshield. The skin on its forehead split and blood poured out. Then it smashed into the windshield again, and its eyes closed.

Juli looked past it to a black woman in her sixties holding a baseball bat. A bloody baseball bat. She wore her hair in tight cornrows and had thick, horn-rimmed glasses. Behind her was a boy in an Orioles t-shirt. He held a rag against his head and had blood running down his face.

The woman scurried to the passenger side door and leaned close to the glass barrier.

"Let us in. Please."

Beyond them, Juli saw the street was overrun by zombies. They descended upon the few living people, who were attacked, eaten, and reanimated.

"I'm begging you! Please!"

Juli hit the unlock button, and the woman jerked open the rear passenger door. She pushed the boy in first, then climbed in behind him.

"I'm Juli."

The woman peered at her through the gaps in the front seats.

"That's nice. Now, how about you get us the hell out of here."

Juli put the vehicle in reverse and backed up as quickly as she felt comfortable going between the narrow walls. In her mirror, she saw the cop she'd earlier run over. He crawled toward them, dragging himself along the pavement with his hands. The bum was now on his feet and sprinting toward them.

Juli hit the cop first. The bumper connected with his face with a hard smack. Then she hit the bum, who careened off the SUV, hit the wall, and bounced back into the path of the vehicle. The Audi bounced up and down, up and down, as the front and rear wheels rolled over him.

Juli glanced at the woman. "Sorry about that."

The woman shook her head. "Honey, you ain't got to apologize for nothing if you can get us out of the city."

"I'll do my best."

They exited the alley, and Juli turned back in the direction from which she'd entered the town. They passed by the same buildings, which were now fully engulfed in flames. Several burning zombies shambled along the streets. Two zombies, charred black like chicken after a grilling mishap, ate a soldier who still had a flame thrower strapped to his back.

"It's the end of days..." the woman whispered.

"What?"

She looked away from the death and to Juli. "Nothing. Don't mind me, Miss. I'm Helen." She patted the boy on his thigh. "And this is Jeremy. My grandson."

Jeremy didn't look up.

"What happened to him?"

Helen pulled Jeremy's hand off the rag on his cheek, but the rag stuck fast. She peeled it away, and it ripped like Velcro.

"Police whooped him a good one." She gently pressed down on a bloody wound on the boy's cheek. Juli thought she could see bone underneath it. He let his head rest against the window and took shallow, ragged breaths.

"Should we go to a hospital? For help?"

Helen stared out the window at the city that was falling around them. "No... No, honey. I do believe we're on our own, now."

As Juli drove on, she realized the old woman was correct.

CHAPTER FOURTEEN

"I SAID DROP YOUR PANTS, BITCH!"

Ramey stared down the black barrel of the shotgun, then allowed her eyes to refocus beyond it and on the face of the man who wanted to rape and kill her, not necessarily in that order.

She considered pleading, begging, trying to reason with him: the things she always saw people do on TV shows, but that seemed as pointless as her half-eaten Snickers. Instead, she unbuckled her belt.

Danny watched with fevered, glassy eyes. Yellow pus oozed from his tear ducts.

Ramey pulled the belt free of the denim loops and let it drop to the floor.

"That's a good start. Now, keep going."

Ramey took her time as she unzipped her jeans. While his eyes were locked on her crotch, she watched Danny. His lips quivered, and his mouth twisted into a sneer.

"Hurry it up."

The zipper reached the end of the line. Her jeans sagged open in a yawning V that revealed her light pink panties.

Danny scurried out from behind the glass counter. He was three feet away from her, and Ramey felt heat coming off him like a radiator.

He got closer, a foot away, and now Ramey could smell the air being expelled from his gaping mouth. It smelled sour, like spoiled hamburger. When he pushed himself against her, she had to fight off the urge to puke all over him. Maybe I should, she thought. But he still wielded the shotgun, and angering him seemed unwise.

Danny took his left hand and reached under her shirt. His hot, moist flesh groped the skin on her belly, then continued up as he squeezed her breast through her bra so hard that she groaned.

The sick man mistook the sound for pleasure, and he grunted, expelling another mouthful of fetid air into her nostrils. He leaned into her and pushed his face against hers. Ramey felt drool seeping from his mouth and onto her cheeks, where it slithered down her face like molasses.

I'm gonna barf. It's gonna happen.

But she stopped herself through sheer willpower. Mind over matter, Ramey. If you don't mind, it doesn't matter.

She felt his hardness as he pressed his crotch against her naval, and his breaths came faster. He removed his left hand from her chest and took it on a detour to the southern border, where his fingers slid into the waistline of her panties and fumbled around in clumsy exploration.

Ramey gritted her teeth as he poked and prodded with his fingers, but then he changed course. He took the elastic of her underwear and yanked them halfway down her thighs. He dropped the shotgun, which clattered against the tile floor as he lowered his sweatpants. In her peripheral vision, she saw his dick spring free and bob up and down like a buoy on rough seas.

He's going to fuck you if you don't do something, she told herself. Are you going to stand there like some helpless damsel in distress and let him?

He pressed against her, his hips thrusting as he attempted to enter her. He bounced off her left hip, then her abdomen, then the crease where her crotch met her thigh. Ramey noticed he was staring at their genitals, trying to aim. This was her chance to escape this mess. She had to take it.

She swung her arms and clawed at his face. Fortunately, her aim was better than Danny's. Much better. She looped fingers through each of his stretched earlobes, balled her hands into fists, and jerked her arms downward.

Ramey felt the skin stretch in her hands, and it reminded her of pulling on rubber bands. The heavy-duty, extra wide ones, though, not the standard issue type you shot like little bullets. This took effort.

Danny screamed. His right fist connected with her upper lip, and she felt the skin break and hot blood flood her mouth. But she refused to let go. She pulled harder. Violent. Triumphant.

The flesh of his earlobes stretched further, then snapped and ripped away. Ramey's hands came free with two silver rings and two long tendrils of bloody flesh that snaked and curled around her fingers.

Danny stumbled backward and crashed against the display case, grabbing the sides of his head. Blood gushed through his fingers. "You bitch! I'm gonna get you now, you bitch!"

But he didn't move his hands away from his shredded ears. Ramey realized he was crying, but the tears were an obscene mix of pus and blood that decorated his cheeks like war paint.

Ramey dove sideways toward the shotgun and grabbed it. When she climbed to her knees and spun to Danny, he was coming at her, his dick now flaccid and dangling.

Guess I killed the mood.

She didn't stop to think because, if she did, she might have stopped herself. Instead, Ramey pulled the trigger.

She wasn't prepared for the force of the 10 gauge. Neither was Danny. The recoil blew the gun out of her hands and threw Ramey backward. She fell over upended display racks, and a mound of snack bags broke her fall. If her ears hadn't been ringing like a school bell, she would have heard them pop under her weight.

Danny wasn't as lucky. He was less than five feet away from the end of the barrel when the slug caught him in the upper chest. The shot sent him flying into the glass counter behind him. It shattered on impact, raining glass down like confetti.

Ramey watched, mouth agape, as pints of blood poured from a one-inch hole between the knobs of Danny's collar bones. His eyes remained open in a perpetual state of shock.

Her shoulder was a ball of misery— especially where the shotgun had collided with it—and the pain radiated across her chest. She climbed onto her knees, careful not to push up with her right arm.

She made it to her feet and approached Danny, who sat there, motionless. She pushed against his stomach with her foot to see if there was any reaction. Danny responded by folding over at the waist and the change of position revealed a ragged hole in his back large enough to fit a gallon jug.

She was pissed off and scared and felt sick to her stomach. She didn't mind dispatching the zombies, but this was a person. A living person. And even if he was an aspiring rapist, now she was a killer, and she hated him for that. For turning her into that.

"Damn you. Why were you such an asshole?"

She wiped tears from her eyes and, in doing so, felt her swollen upper lip. She checked her reflection in a sunglasses display rack and saw a half-inch gash to the left of the center. Blood still oozed from the wound. Her reflection helped disperse her inner turmoil, at least a bit.

Ramey grabbed a handful of plastic shopping bags and recommenced gathering food and supplies. She couldn't care less about stealing anymore. She'd earned this bounty.

With three bags full, she moved toward the doorway, stopping when she heard glass crunch behind her.

"I'm not going to look. Nope, not gonna do it."

But the sound grew closer, and, soon, a serenade of low groans joined it.

"Damn it."

Ramey turned around and discovered Danny lurching toward her. Light peeked through the ragged hole in his chest. When he groaned, blood bubbled from the wound.

"You've got to be shitting me," Ramey said. She had seen people bit by zombies turn into the creatures, but Danny the rapist had died from natural causes. Well, as natural as a shotgun blast to the chest could be. She'd expected him to stay dead and had no interest in round two.

As Danny stumbled over spilled groceries and tumbled to his knees, Ramey took her bags and scooted out of the store. When she reached the truck, she considered taking Stan's pistol and finishing him off, but her body ached. She decided to get back on the road instead.

CHAPTER FIFTEEN

THE MORNING SUN SLICED THROUGH THE CLEAR SKY AND heated up the day fast. Grady wasn't certain when the night had succumbed to day. He and Josiah had been walking nonstop.

He wasn't even aware that his bare feet were bleeding and leaving a trail of red footsteps behind him as he traveled. They'd escaped the city, passing by zombies and rioters, police and military. In the chaos, Grady and his dead son were invisible.

He only realized it was daylight after being blinded by a gleaming, white mirage ahead of him. This is *the* light, he thought. We're walking into the light. Into salvation. He picked up the pace, moving at a trot now, and Josiah toddled along beside, still holding Grady's hand.

They were ten feet from the light when Grady's eyes adjusted, and he realized he was actually looking at a silver tractor-trailer parked haphazardly across the roadway. Painted on the side was "East Coast Grocers." Grady shielded his eyes so that the light reflecting off the rig would stop blinding him. When he did, he saw the tall man standing in front of the tractor.

He was a beanpole with white hair pulled back in a long ponytail.

He held a cigarette in one hand and his dick in the other as he pissed in the middle of the street. He was in mid-stream when he saw Grady and the boy.

"Oh, fuckeroo." He tried to shove his manhood back into his pants, urinating all over his hand and jeans in the process. He wiped his hand on his shirt. "I'm sorry, buddy. Thought I had the world to myself out here."

He extended the hand he'd just pissed on, and Grady shook it anyway. "Ross Hillstrom." He peered into the rising sun and was unable to see the man and boy in detail.

"I'm Grady. This is my son, Josiah." Grady patted the boy on the shoulder and could feel him straining to get at Ross. He struggled to hold him back, trying to appear normal and relaxed.

Ross didn't notice anything amiss. If Grady had been the type to dabble in drugs, he'd have known the cigarette in Ross's hand didn't contain tobacco. The man was high as the proverbial kite.

"Where you coming from and where you going?"

"We lived in Baltimore. As for where we're going... Wherever the good Lord takes us, I suppose."

"Well, call me Jesus Christ Almighty then. I've got plenty of room and hate riding solo."

The blaspheme cut Grady's heart like a blade, but he didn't address it. Now that he'd emerged from his stupor, he felt the searing pain in his feet.

Worried and scared, he checked Josiah's and saw the skin around the perimeters was torn and ragged but not bleeding yet. Maybe God had sent this man to rescue them.

"Is that yours?" he asked, motioning to the tractor-trailer.

Ross shrugged. "Sorta, kinda. I was following it down 70 outta Hagerstown. All of a sudden, it stopped right there in the middle of the interstate. I walked up to the cab to check on the driver, and when I opened the door, he jumped out and attacked me.

“I had a hell of a time getting him off me, but after fighting a while, I shoved him over the guardrails and down an embankment. The sucker was trying to bite me!"

He gave a low, slow whistle out of the gap between his front teeth. "Bout that same time, all a Hell was breaking loose. Cars crashing. People fighting. People turning into zombies. Someone rear-ended my pickup and smashed it all to shit, and I figured the fella who'd been driving this wouldn't be needing it anymore, so I hopped in and skidooted out of there. Figured, if nothing else, I'll be able to drive a hell of a long time without running out of food."

Ross turned toward the truck and waved the others forward. "There's a nice sleeper in the back of the cab. Your boy can crash back there. Looks sorta tired."

Grady looked down at Josiah, whose head lolled back and forth. "I appreciate that. I'm sure he could use a nap."

Josiah didn't want to nap. He squirmed and writhed when Grady carried him into the sleeper and kept trying to get at Ross, who was completely clueless about the goings on.

Grady didn't want a repeat of the incident with O'Dell and LaRon, so he used bungee cords he found in the cab to tie Josiah fast to the bed. The boy fought against the restraints, and Grady leaned down and kissed his cold forehead.

"Hush now. Be calm." Josiah listened. For a while.

LESS THAN AN HOUR passed before Ross had to make another stop. "Why don't you and your boy stretch your legs and give the weasel a good shake, too."

Grady didn't need to stretch his legs or shake his weasel, but he didn't want to do anything to raise suspicions. Not that Ross was overly perceptive. Earlier, when he heard Josiah growling in the backseat, Grady used asthma as the excuse. The older man bought it without question.

While Ross left to relieve himself, Grady climbed in the sleeper with Josiah, who was more agitated than ever. He snapped at Grady's hands as he loosened the cords and nearly bit him twice. When the boy was free, Grady held him firmly by his neck to control him.

He saw Ross a dozen yards up the empty highway, smoking and pissing simultaneously. When Ross saw them, he gave a wide, jovial wave. Grady waved back with one hand and held Josiah with the other.

Grady moved so that the truck blocked Ross's view, then knelt on the road and looked into Josiah's face. All the color had left it, and his skin had taken on an almost transparent quality. He could see the crisscrossed jumble of veins under his flesh. They were black. Josiah lunged for him and came within less than an inch of taking off the tip of Grady's nose.

"Josiah, that's bad. Very bad!" he scolded, and Josiah's head drooped like a whipped mule.

A ragged growl fell out of the boy's open mouth. "Hrar graah."

Hungry? Did he just say he's hungry?

Grady looked at his son as drool ran from the boy's gaping mouth. He touched his fingertips to Josiah's chin and lifted it so that the boy's face tilted upward, parallel to his own.

"Are you hungry, Josiah?"

Grady got his answer when Josiah growled again. The poor boy was probably starving. He had eaten little of his hamburger helper the day prior and had nothing since then. But he was beyond hamburger helper now. Grady knew what Josiah wanted. What Josiah needed. God had given him back his son, and now it was his duty to fulfill his needs.

He rolled up his shirt sleeve to reveal the soft, fatty skin under his upper arm. He'd seen what happened when these dead souls ate from the still living, but Christ himself had told his disciples to partake of his flesh. Now, Grady believed it was his turn.

"Eat, my son."

Josiah lunged for his arm and buried his teeth into his father's skin. Grady let his eyes fall shut and tried to stay still as Josiah ate.

CHAPTER SIXTEEN

Mead planned to head West. He had no particular destination in mind, but he knew the population grew sparser once you passed Missouri. He thought he might eventually aim for Wyoming or Idaho or any of those states no one visited unless they were born there.

He'd made it forty miles when the Cavalier's engine blew. A bang loud enough to make his body vibrate exploded, and all forward motion suddenly ceased. Blue smoke seeped out from the gaps around the hood.

"Aw, fuck!" Mead knew the Cav was nearing the end of its life, but he hadn't seen a car on the road for fifteen miles. Walking a marathon hoping to find a new ride was low on his priority list.

He sat in the car until the smoke became heavy enough to burn his lungs. He grabbed the hockey sticks and started emptying the food from the trunk when the front of the car burst into flames. My shitty assed luck, he thought.

He grabbed an armload of junk food before the heat became too much to bear. Then he walked half a football field up the road, sat on the berm, and ate chips while he watched it burn.

Bundy saw the smoke billowing above the tree line in the distance. He assumed a house or small town might be burning, but when he got closer, he saw the coupe consumed in flames.

He drove around it and tried to see if anyone was inside, but it appeared empty. Just as well as orange flames filled the interior. Anyone inside would be charbroiled and well done.

That thought made him hungry. Before this plague and before prison, he'd been something of a grill aficionado. He owned several varieties and had been a blue ribbon winner at the county fair four years running for his pulled pork.

Aside from weekend barbecuing adventures, Bundy had spent much of his life managing a warehouse that sold parts for things like weed eaters and lawn mowers. His job was monotonous but easy enough as far as nine-to-fives go. He got along well with his co-workers and bosses but never considered them friends. Bundy didn't really have friends, but he had plenty of acquaintances, and that sufficed.

I had a good life, he thought. He hoped he could build another one in this new wasteland.

After he passed the car, he saw a person sitting further up the road. He thought it was a woman with long brown hair, but he soon realized his mistake. This was a man, albeit a homely one.

Bundy flicked off the safety on the pistol he had holstered at his side and stepped out of the van.

That's the biggest motherfucker I've ever seen, Mead thought as Bundy strolled toward him. He wondered if sitting on the ground had skewed his perception, so he jumped to his feet. *Nope, still fucking huge.*

The giant had a large, open face that seemed as easy to read as a grade school primer. That coupled with his straw blond hair made him look like an oversized toddler. Mead considered brandishing one of his double-bladed sticks but decided against it, hoping to make a better first impression.

"I'm Mead." He extended his hand, not because he was ever big on handshakes but because it seemed like the polite thing to do.

"Bundy." The giant's hand swallowed up Mead's own.

"That your first name or your last?"

"Neither. But that's what everyone calls me."

"Then I will, too."

Bundy motioned to the fireball that used to be a car. "That your ride?"

"It was. Still is, I guess. Not that it'll do me any good now."

Bundy nodded. "No. I'd say its usefulness has been fully expended." He eyed Mead's customized weapons. "You make those?"

Mead squatted and grabbed one. He held it up for display but didn't hand it over. "Yeah. The stick is supposed to be unbreakable. So far, that's held up."

"Nice." Bundy tapped the firearm at his side. "I'm not too quick, so I prefer something I can use at a distance."

"I've never even shot a gun. Besides, I don't really trust them in an emergency."

"Understandable. Firearms are best left out of the hands of the inexperienced."

Bundy's gigantic upper arms hung loose from his sleeveless shirt. They were the size of country hams and perfect for eating if you were a zombie. Mead didn't know if the man would appreciate unsolicited advice but tendered it anyway.

"I hope I'm not overstepping my bounds, but you might want to put on a shirt with sleeves. Denim if you have it."

Bundy looked from his arms to Mead. "Why's that?"

Mead was excited to share his knowledge. His voice quickened. "You've seen the zombies eating people?"

Bundy nodded.

"They tear through bare skin like it's raw burger. Cotton and poly aren't much better. But denim or leather, they're going to have to gnaw away for a hell of a long time to get through that and bite you."

"Okay..."

"And you need gloves. If you get into a hand-to-hand kind of situation, all it takes is a half second where you're pushing them away or fighting them off for them to chomp down on your finger and—" He smacked his hands together. "Bang! You're a ticking zombie time bomb!" Mead ran his own gloved hands over his body, displaying the heavy material and the duct tape he'd supplemented it with. "See what I mean? Everything covered. You've got to protect yourself, man."

Bundy raised an eyebrow but didn't respond further.

They waited through an uncomfortable silence that was broken only when Bundy noticed Mead staring longingly at his van.

"Where are you heading?" Bundy asked.

"How about wherever you're going?"

Bundy nodded again. "Get in. Only rule I got is don't be annoying."

"That I can do," Mead assured him. It ended up being a false promise.

Shortly after they fled Pennsylvania, boredom overcame them, and they stopped in a small Maryland border town where they held a contest to see who could kill the most zombies in sixty seconds. The center of town seemed a suitable site as several dozen creatures roamed freely.

Mead, armed with his hockey stick, went first as Bundy checked his watch. Mead strolled toward the zombies, stuck his index and middle fingers into his mouth, and let out a shrill whistle. "Time to die, motherfuckers!"

All the zombies were of the slower variety. That's something

Mead had noticed over the last few days. Almost all of them seemed to have slowed down. He only witnessed one runner after day three, and that was a man Mead saw get attacked and turn.

When Mead whistled, the zombies headed in his direction. The leader of the pack was a beefy senior citizen, and with one swing of the stick, Mead sliced his head open diagonally from his jowls to his eyebrows.

Next up was a teenage girl in a Catholic school uniform. Mead took a moment to admire how the swells of her breasts pushed against the white material of her shirt, then remembered this was a race. He used the knife end of the stick to pierce her eye socket.

He felled another eighteen zombies in the minute. The last one was a police officer, and after Mead brought the bladed end of the stick down squarely on the top of his head, opening a crevice through which the man's dead brains were visible, Buddy yelled, "Time!"

"I was hoping I'd get that one," Bundy added.

Mead dropped back to the van. He felt good about his performance and hoped he'd impressed the big man. He wanted his respect. He felt like he'd earned it.

The zombies were thicker now, drawn by the commotion. Bundy took his spot at the front of the vehicle and leaned back against the hood. Mead felt the front end sag.

"Ready?" Bundy asked.

"Whenever you are."

"Go."

Bundy drew his pistol, raised it, and aimed. He plinked a woman in a "World's Greatest Mom!" shirt first. Then a boy in a soccer uniform, then a middle-aged man who had most of his face eaten away. He hit three more, all headshots, before firing a round that went through the cheek of a woman in a lime green pantsuit and flew out the other side.

"Almost got a hole in one!" Mead called out.

Bundy aimed again, and, that time, the bullet stuck beside her eye, and the left side of her face blew out. He killed two more, and his magazine was empty. No problem, he thought as he smoothly expelled it and replaced it with another from his pocket.

He was hurrying, though, and his first shot went wide. Bundy got back on his game and shot and killed seven in a row. He hit the eighth in the throat, but it kept coming. He used another round to kill it. He offed a woman in yoga pants with his last round. Bundy had a few seconds left but needed to reload magazines, so he was done.

"Seventeen." Bundy said. "You got me."

"Not by much. You're a hell of a shot."

"You should see me with a rifle. Used to do thousand-yard shooting for fun."

"A thousand yards? Holy shit. You could stand here and kill zombies back in Pennsylvania."

Bundy chuckled and climbed back into the van. "Want to finish them off?"

Another dozen zombies remained on the road ahead of them.

"With pleasure."

Mead dispatched them with ease, but in the process, he completely decapitated one of the creatures. As the severed head tumbled through the air like a wobbly football, black blood flew into Mead's ridiculously long hair.

When he finished, he joined Bundy in the van and grabbed some partially used napkins from the floor. He used them to wring the gore from his locks, then tossed the bloodied paper onto the floor. Bundy looked at him and shook his head. More zombies wandered toward them, but the road was clear, so the men let them be.

CHAPTER SEVENTEEN

When the hospital elevator reached the ground floor, the doors opened to chaos in the lobby. Nurses were eating patients. Patients were eating visitors. A janitor munched on the meaty arm of a man who could only be a high-ranking hospital executive, judging by his expensive suit.

Mina couldn't count the number of zombies, but by some miracle, all of them were too busy devouring other people to notice her. She kept tight against the walls and made it to the exit before being spotted.

She might have made a clean break if the automatic sliding glass doors hadn't created a ruckus by slamming into a dying paramedic. The paramedic screamed, and every zombie in the lobby looked in his direction.

Mina was less than five feet away and directly in their line of sight. She sprinted for the open doors, almost tripping over a patient on a stretcher. When she stumbled into it, she saw the patient strapped to it was dead. Even though a neck brace held its head in place, its jaws snapped at her.

The other zombies were coming for her. She shoved the stretcher at them, then sprinted into the warm daylight. Despite her father coming back to life, despite the bloodbath in the hospital, Mina expected to find safety outside. It was similar to how she had always expected her father to wake up and be kind. Somehow, despite a life filled with pain and disappointment, Mina remained an optimist.

The zombies on the street raced for her as soon as her feet struck the sidewalk. I'm going to die, she thought. She was finally free of her father's torture only to die a few hours later. That must be her punishment for wishing him dead. Her life would end before she had time to enjoy herself.

She glanced back at the hospital where the automatic doors had opened again, and zombies rushed out. The zombies on the street also moved in her direction. She considered closing her eyes and waiting for death when she heard an engine running. She turned toward the sound and saw an ambulance idling underneath a sign labeled "Admissions."

The ambulance was ten yards away, but it looked like a mile as Mina rushed toward it. The growls of the chasing zombies drowned out her pounding footsteps. She could smell the sickness on them, like fever sweats and rotten potatoes mixed together. The odor became overwhelming the closer they got to her.

As she grabbed the handle and pulled the ambulance door open, she felt a zombie at her back. It grabbed onto her hair, and her head snapped. She yanked her head forward and felt her hair slip free from its bloody hands as she dove into the ambulance head first.

Mina quickly grabbed the door to pull it closed, but as she did, a zombie got its arm in between the door and the frame. The metal squashed the appendage with a crunch that made Mina think of stepping on a potato chip. She opened and closed the door again, and, this time, a squishing sound accompanied the crunch. One more try, and the door tore through the zombie's forearm. Its hand fell inside the ambulance, and outside, the zombie battered the window with its stump.

Mina grabbed the shifter and was ready to throw the van into drive when a symphony of tinkling glass and clanging metal in the back stole her attention. She spun in the seat and looked behind her. That's when she saw the zombie in a paramedic's uniform. He'd pulled a drawer of medicines and medical instruments onto himself and was covered in them as he sprawled on the floor.

Glass vials broke underneath the zombie as it rolled aimlessly and tried to get off its back and to its feet. The pile of fallen debris complicated that task. To Mina, it looked like a turtle someone had sat upside down on its shell.

Through the windshield, Mina saw dozens of zombies swarming toward her. She searched the dash and the storage compartments for anything she could use as a weapon. In the glove box, she found a box of insulin syringes. She ripped open the box and tore the packaging off one of them. After removing the cover, she saw the needle was less than half an inch long and about as thick as a strand of hair.

"Oh, damn. Damn it all!"

"It's gonna get ya, Birdie," she heard her father's voice shout inside her head. "You ain't getting out of this alive."

While she looked for a better option, the paramedic zombie heard her. More glass broke, and more equipment went flying as it flailed. Soon, it had cleared enough space so that it could roll onto its belly. Then it climbed to its knees and crawled toward the front of the bus.

When it growled, it got Mina's attention. She looked back. The paramedic was two feet away. The man had several large bite marks on his arms and still wore his blue, protective latex gloves. It growled again, and Mina could smell the death coming from its mouth.

The zombie swatted at her and caught Mina's bare arm in its hand. She felt the coldness coming through the glove. The zombie squeezed hard, putting deep divots in her skin, but the glove prevented his nails from breaking Mina's skin.

Mina tried to pull away but couldn't, and she settled on holding it back instead. "You're gonna die, Birdie. Deserve it, too, after what you did to me. Kill your own daddy with a piss pot of all things. Dirty Birdie."

"Screw you, Daddy!" Mina said to the voice in her head. It had renewed her strength, and with her free hand, she reached for the syringe she'd set aside. As she felt for it, she looked up at the zombie, its dead eyes staring back. They looked like they'd been blue once. She found the syringe and gripped it in her fist.

Mina knew she had one chance, and she aimed carefully. The needle slid into the zombie's right eye. Nothing happened initially, then fluid oozed out.

Mina kept pushing until she felt the needle hit resistance and break. She left the syringe jutting from the monster's eye and felt for another. She found the box but couldn't free the syringe from its paper wrapper with one hand. Mina put it to her mouth and ripped the packaging off with her teeth.

Pink vitreous fluid from the zombie's right eye dripped down the syringe and onto Mina's cheek. She spat out the syringe's packaging, then used her mouth to pull off the cap.

With a quick jab, Mina pierced the zombie's left eye with the new needle. With both eyes blinded, the paramedic released Mina and flailed wildly. Mina shoved it backward, where it landed in a heap of supplies and equipment. Both syringes jutted from its eye sockets, and it fell over and over again each time it tried to rise.

Ahead, zombies had clogged the street from one side to the other. She checked her mirrors, and only a dozen or so looked to be behind her. When she shifted into reverse and hit the gas, she heard the big, boxy vehicle slam into the creatures. One went under the tires, and she felt them spin. She hit the gas but didn't move.

"No you don't. Not now." She grabbed the four-wheel-drive stick and engaged it. When she hit the gas, the ambulance lurched, then rolled over the zombies on the ground. She kept backing up until she'd cleared a fifteen-foot-long path, then did a three-point turn in the street and headed in the opposite direction of the main horde.

She ran over a few more zombies but was soon clear of them. Mina didn't know where to go. Escaping the hospital seemed like accomplishment enough. As her daddy said, everything else was gravy.

CHAPTER EIGHTEEN

Emory's second crash was, thankfully, less violent than the first. When the Bronco hit the zombies, the soft mass of them absorbed the momentum. Bodies bounced and crunched, but the Bronco itself came to a slow stop and was unscathed aside from a few fresh dents and a crinkled hood.

He felt his heart racing and worried for a moment that he might be on the precipice of another coronary event. Wim reached over and rested his strong hand on his shoulder.

"Are you all right?"

Emory nodded and deliberately slowed his breathing. "I am. Thank you for asking."

"It was my own fault for driving too fast. I'm sorry."

"No apologies necessary, Wim." Emory stared through the windshield, where a dozen or so zombies remained. "Do you think we can drive through them?"

Wim followed his gaze. "Maybe."

Emory felt the Bronco creep forward. It only made it a few inches before stopping. Wim pushed the gas pedal to the floor, and the engine roared, but the vehicle didn't move.

"I do believe we are trapped," Emory said.

Wim nodded. "Mmm hmm." He rummaged through the backseat.

While he did that, Emory watched the zombies press against the truck. They had them surrounded now. Emory flicked on the dome light and could see their faces squashed against the windows. Their hands clawed desperately at the glass.

A young woman stared at him. Half of her head was shaved, and the word "Faithful" was tattooed on her neck. Emory tried to look past her death and into the person she had been.

No humanity remained in her eyes, but that didn't change the fact that she'd been as alive as Wim and himself recently. He imagined her standing in a mosh pit in a concert, banging her head or crowd-surfing or whatever the punk crowd was into these days.

To her right was an older man, but one still younger than Emory himself. He wore glasses with lenses so thick they magnified his eyes and turned him into something of a caricature. He wore a suit but one straight off the rack. Emory thought he could be an accountant or, perhaps, an actuary. Something boring but important.

Further back, a priest, whose white collar was stained red by blood, tried to fight his way through the crowd. He still clutched rosary beads in one hand, but the other was a wild claw, slashing and lashing out at everything around him.

If you allowed yourself, it was easy to forget these were people. Too easy. Emory supposed it to be a necessary coping mechanism. One vital to surviving their plight and not dissolving into a puddle of anxiety and distress.

If you thought of them as monsters, it was easier to fight them. To kill them. Although that was something he had yet to do and hoped to avoid for as long as possible.

He'd left all the killing to poor Wim, and while he admired the farmer's capabilities, he wondered what would happen if Wim allowed himself to stop and think. Emory almost hoped that never happened. That Wim might never look at them and see the life of the dead.

Wim emerged with a pistol that had a long, skinny barrel. "You might want to cover your ears. This is apt to be loud."

Emory plugged his ear canals with his fingers and watched Wim roll down the driver's side window just enough to push out the barrel. Then, he started shooting.

I'm sorry, Emory thought as they fell under the hail of gunfire. I know this must be done, but I'm sorry for what you've become.

He realized that he wasn't certain which "you" he meant. The zombies, or Wim and himself. There were no heroes in this violent, dangerous world. No victors in the battle between the living and the dead.

CHAPTER NINETEEN

He said his name was Ted Dash and declared himself a retired Navy SEAL, but the more he talked, the less Jorge was inclined to believe anything he said. Still, his assault rifle ("Converted it to full auto myself"), complete with a seventy-round drum magazine ("Bought it on the dark web from a little Chinaman"), meant that when Dash spoke, Bolivar listened.

Dash said he'd come to Dover AFB to "Volunteer to kill the zombie motherfuckers." He'd arrived a few hours before Bolivar and, as he told the story, "Found the gates locked tighter than a nun's snatch. Didn't see no one left alive. Really alive, I mean, of course. Just those zombie fuckers." He pointed to the dead soldiers.

"So I kilt em. Didn't feel right, exactly, shooting fellow soldiers, but I figured I was doin' 'em a favor. I wouldn't want to be walking around like that, killing people and eatin' their skin for all of eternity. Nope, not me. So I figured it was a mercy killin'."

Dash said he ran out of gas three miles from the base and jogged the rest of the way. Bolivar half expected him to steal his car, not that it was actually his, but instead, Dash asked for a ride.

"Where you headin'?" Dash asked.

Bolivar struggled for an answer and came up blank. "I'm not sure."

"Way I see it, D.C.'s the best option."

"Why do you think that?"

"Cause of the President and shit. They got to be evacuating everyone."

Bolivar considered telling him what had happened to Philadelphia but decided to keep that bit of information to himself.

DASH WAS PUSHING FIFTY, and his high and tight had gone gray. He was tall and fit with only the slightest beginnings of a gut. His tanned skin was so brown it looked like shoe leather. He was full of tales of covert missions in exotic Latin American locations and heroic escapades overthrowing dictators, pairing up with drug cartels, and bedding native women. Jorge doubted all of it, but the chatter helped pass the time as the situation outside the car deteriorated.

Zombies had overrun the nation's capital. Many wore suits; former lobbyists, aides, or maybe even members of congress. Others had been tourists, complete with novelty tee-shirts and cameras that still hung from straps around their necks. Together, they formed enormous crowds—a zombie version of a march on the city—and filled the streets from side to side. Jorge was forced to make detours through alleyways and side streets to avoid the masses of them.

"It's gone," Bol said. "We have to get out of here."

Dash stared out the windows of the car and clenched his AK so tight that his knuckles went snow white. "Keep drivin', brother. Get us to the White House, then we'll decide."

When they rolled on to Pennsylvania Avenue, Bolivar parked the car at the cylindrical barriers that blocked motor vehicles from driving past the White House. Zombies shuffled around the two blocks in front of the iconic building.

"Satisfied?" Bol asked.

Instead of answering, Dash opened his car door and stepped into the diminishing orange light of the afternoon.

"Come on! Don't go out there!" Bolivar yelled.

Dash marched away from the car, raising the AK to his shoulder. "I gotta see it for myself."

Against all his instincts, Bolivar exited the car and followed. There were a few dozen zombies in the street, but they wandered aimlessly and weren't packed together like they had been in other parts of the city.

As they stumbled about, they careened off of fences and discarded bicycles and kiosks that had once sold cheap trinkets. Bol realized the reason there were fewer monsters here was because they couldn't easily maneuver through the vehicle barriers.

When Dash was within ten yards of them, he started shooting. Despite his supposed SEAL prowess, his ability to connect with head shots was lacking, and with the rifle on full automatic, he blew through half his magazine and had dropped only fourteen. The relative failure only enraged him, and he sprinted at the creatures, gripping the gun at his waist and firing as he ran.

Bullets whistled through the air. A few connected, mostly with torsos and limbs, but there weren't many lethal hits to the brain. My God, Jorge thought, this guy's not only a blowhard, he's insane.

As if to prove the point, Dash screamed. "Die, you zombie motherfuckers!"

Within seconds, his rifle was empty. He tossed it to the side and pulled a Bowie knife from his belt. Bolivar watched in a mixture of awe and horror as Dash leaped into the air and pounced on the nearest zombie.

He plunged the knife into its face, jerked it free, then stabbed it again. Three more zombies moved toward him, and one of them grabbed Dash's arm.

Bolivar drew his pistol and shot. The bullet hit the zombie in the back of its head and exploded out of its eye socket. He shot the second in its mouth, and it crumpled to the ground.

The third zombie left Dash and came at Bol, but before he could fire, Dash climbed to his feet and jumped onto its back, screaming like a howler monkey. He rammed the blade of the knife into the zombie's eye, then gave the handle an extra twist for good measure. They fell in a heap, and a moment later, Dash slithered out from underneath the dead zombie.

"Good fuckin' shootin', brother!" He wiped zombie blood off his knife and onto the leg of his jeans.

"You're crazy."

"As a shit house rat, brother! As a shit house rat!" He grinned a madman's grin.

He clapped Jorge on the back hard enough to take his breath away, then gazed toward the White House. "Would ya look at that..."

Jorge did. He saw zombies littering the North Lawn. Women in smart business attire. Secret Service agents in jet black suits. Groundskeepers, police, security guards. All of them were dead. All of them were zombies. Several lumbered across the steps of the White House—undead tourists.

"Hey, you think the President got out before he turned into one of those motherfuckers?" Dash asked, snapping Bolivar out of his daze.

Dash's eyes were crazed but gleaming, and Bolivar realized the man was crying.

"I don't know. I'd say the odds are pretty slim."

Dash nodded. Zombies from further up the path were heading toward them.

"We better scoot," Dash said.

The men jogged to the car.

"Hey, when I was enlisted, we used to hear about a thing in West Virginia called Project Greek Island. Ever hear of it?"

Bolivar shook his head as he turned around.

"Yeah. It was some underground bunker big enough to house all the government big wigs in case Khrushchev decided to drop A bombs."

After Philadelphia, Bolivar thought civilization was over. But now? If what Dash said was true, there might be a chance.

"Do you know where it's supposed to be?"

"Sulfur Spring or something like that. Middle of fucking nowhere."

"White Sulphur Springs? There's a huge hotel down there. My C.O. went one summer with his wife's family. Ritzy place from what he said."

"That's the one!" Dash was beaming. Some of the craziness had fled his eyes. "That's the place, brother. The bunker's under the hotel. Carved right into the motherfucking mountain, from what I heard."

"You know how to get there?"

"West?"

Dash's goofy, gap-toothed smile brightened Bolivar's mood and made him forget, momentarily, that the man was a lunatic.

CHAPTER TWENTY

Solomon discovered an old K car sitting outside a gas station with the hose to the pump still inserted into the gas tank. He pulled the nozzle free and cast it aside, where petrol dribbled onto the pavement.

The keys weren't in the ignition, but that didn't matter. One of the many skills he'd picked up over the years was hot-wiring, and, less than twenty seconds after plopping into the driver's seat, the engine was running, and he was on the road.

The fentanyl lolly had turned the pain in his head into an annoying, reverberating drumbeat. Between crashed and abandoned cars and the undead bastards, driving to his shop took three times as long as it should have, but he made it.

He didn't bother stopping to kill any zombies along the way. Even with the ax, he didn't feel comfortable being out in the midst of them. He had other plans for that.

When he pulled in front of the large warehouse, which the sign atop declared "Baldwin Residential & Commercial Construction," it annoyed him to see the bay door to the garage standing half open.

He hadn't visited the shop in nearly a week. He'd been too busy worrying about his whore of a wife (God rest her soul) to stay atop the business. Now, it seemed like the canaries had decided to play while the cat was away.

He exited the car and moved to the open door, where he saw nothing amiss. The colossal Kenworth W900 tri-axel dump truck that had set him back over two hundred thousand dollars filled most of the cavity, but an assortment of other machines and equipment was scattered about. There were no obvious signs of looting, but the open garage door meant someone had been here. He raised the ax, poised to attack.

Saw didn't find anyone in the garage. He let his guard down slightly as he moved into the customer service area. It, too, appeared undisturbed and unoccupied.

He'd almost given up on finding anyone in the building when he heard a thudding noise coming from behind a door labeled "Private." Behind that door was Solomon's office, and, apparently, it was occupied.

The thought enraged him. "You'd be wise to get your thievin' ass out here right now!"

His voice drew another thud, but the door remained closed.

"Sneaky bastard!"

Saw, by nature, was an angry man, but he could usually hold it at bay, at least, for a while. His patience seemed to have vanished.

He stomped across the room, giving no thought to the possibility that whoever was inside might be armed and waiting to punch another hole in his noggin. He was hungry to kill, and nothing else mattered.

As soon as he threw open the door and stepped inside, his feet flew out from under him, and he crashed backward onto the floor. The ax skidded across the room and ended up under an industrial couch, but Solomon didn't notice.

His head cracked against the linoleum, and fresh waves of nauseating pain assailed him. He pushed it aside—as much as possible—and crawled to his knees. He felt slippery wetness under him. It was all over the floor, and he slowed his movement to keep his balance as he climbed to his feet.

Saw half walked, half scooted further into the room. His eyes darted to and fro as he scanned the office, and soon enough, he saw the man behind his desk. He was face down on the floor, and ahead of him was an overturned mop bucket. That's when it all made sense.

"Hector?" The fucking janitor. Still coming to work in the midst of this mess. I really should bump up his pay.

Hector was older than Solomon and spoke almost no English. He was also as illegal as butt-fucking in Iran, but Solomon didn't mind. Half his crew was paid under the table and had questionable backgrounds. Considering his own past, he felt it his duty to give the boys a second chance.

Saw moved closer to the man who tried to rise to his knees, but his hands slipped in the spilled soapy liquid, and he face-planted onto the floor.

"Hold up, mate."

Solomon grabbed him by the back of his chambray work shirt and lifted. When Hector's face came into view, Solomon saw it was broken and bloody. The eyes were closed at first, but they snapped open, and Solomon saw the dead eyes of a zombie.

At the same time, Hector opened his eyes, and his arm lashed out, catching Solomon's jaw. His cool, clumsy fingers scratched at Saw's tongue and fished around inside his mouth.

He thought it felt almost obscene, like he had a mouthful of small writhing cocks. Saw bit down and felt Hector's skin tear. His teeth met phalanges. He kept biting.

Dead Hector tried to pull his hand free, and that repositioned his middle finger so that the joint sat between Solomon's teeth. He chomped harder and felt it give way. He allowed Hector to fall, and the man took another nosedive. Saw spat the janitor's finger to the floor, where it seemed to point at him accusingly.

"Fuck you, too, pal."

Solomon slid backward, soaking the seat of his pants. The cold water helped clear his head. When he saw Hector crawling toward him, he knew it was time to finish him once and for all. Saw scanned the room for the ax but didn't see it anywhere. He considered smashing the janitor's head with his foot but didn't trust that on the water-slick linoleum. He needed a weapon, and he found one.

Saw grabbed the mop and put the wood handle to his knee. When he pressed his weight against it, it responded with a satisfying crack. He tossed the mop head aside.

Hector was only a few feet away now, and Saw aimed the broken, jagged end in his direction. He let the janitor get another foot closer. As Hector growled at him, Solomon thrust the mop handle at his face. The wood sunk deep into Hector's nasal cavity.

Hector's body went limp, his head suspended by the stick. Solomon almost dropped the handle but then decided to bounce it back and forth, laughing as the dead man moved like a puppet in a Punch and Judy show. That lasted a full minute before he lost interest.

Afterward, Solomon returned to the garage, then he closed and locked the bay door. He had a plan, but it would take time to do it right. He gathered together several long poles of rebar and a welding torch. Time to go to work.

CHAPTER TWENTY-ONE

THE VAN RAN OUT OF GAS SOON AFTER THEY CROSSED INTO West Virginia. Mead and Bundy had been heading south with intentions of venturing into the mountains, which Bundy assured Mead were sparsely populated. Bundy also assured him they had another thirty miles worth of gas in the tank when the engine sputtered, then stopped in the middle of a generic small town.

"It's nothing to get your panties bunched up over," Bundy said with the sort of casual indifference that got Mead's heart beating so hard he could hear it in his ears. The big man was a crack shot, that was for sure, but he was so... relaxed. Mead couldn't help but get pissed off. This is the end of the fucking world. Start acting like it.

Bundy fished a garden hose out of the back of the van and held it up like he'd just won first place in the Pinewood Derby. Mead knew the look because he watched the other kids get their trophies while he sat on the sidelines with his shitty eighth-place car in his lap.

Bundy added a five-gallon gas can. "Problem solved."

Mead looked up and down the street. Two zombies, both twenty yards away, seemed to ignore them. Bundy handed Mead the hose and the red plastic container.

"Why do I have to get the gas?"

"It's my van. You've been freeloading thus far. Time to earn your keep."

He looked dead serious, which pissed Mead off even more. Then Bundy laughed and clapped him on the shoulder so hard that Mead thought he might topple over like a Weeble.

"I'm just joshing ya. You get the gas, and I'll cover your ass. Sound fair?" He took out a rifle to demonstrate his end of the deal. Mead had no idea what kind of gun it was, but the barrel was long, and it had a scope big enough you could probably see alien turds on the moon through it.

"Okay," Mead said as he headed up the road to the nearest car—a bright yellow Pontiac Sunfire. He flipped open the gas cover, then unscrewed the cap, which he dropped to the pavement. He kicked it down the street, past Bundy.

The plastic bounced and hopped before coming to a stop outside a flower kiosk that was too far away for the men to hear the groan that followed.

Gas fumes assaulted his nostrils as Mead inserted the hose into the gas tank. He held the hose to his lips and sucked cautiously. Nothing happened. He tried again with the same result.

"Must be empty!" he called out to Bundy, who had rested the rifle across the hood of the van in a sniper's position.

"You ain't sipping soda. You gotta suck on it. Pretend you're back at summer camp playing doctor with your boyfriend!"

Bundy laughed. Mead did not. *Fuck you, jerk. You're the one that was probably gobbling cock in prison a week ago, not me.*

Mead sucked like he was trying to drink the thickest milkshake of all time and was rewarded with a mouthful of gasoline. He coughed and sucked it down his throat and into his nasal passages, where it burned like liquid fire.

He puked it onto the pavement, his eyes watering. And all he could hear was Bundy chortling so hard that Mead thought the fat bastard might have the big one right there. He almost hoped he would.

"Hurry up," Bundy said between guffaws. "You're losing it!"

Mead looked down to find gas gushing from the hose and all over his shoes. He quickly stuck the hose in the gas can and waited for it to fill.

Inside the clapboard flower booth, a zombie crawled out from under a pile of dead roses and lilies. She had been pushing retirement age and wore a green apron and visor cap with "MeeMaw's Meadow" embroidered in white thread. Her glasses sat askew on her face, but she was past needing them anymore.

Gas bubbled from the can, and Mead pulled the hose free from the Pontiac. Bundy moved to the van's gas tank and inserted a funnel. Neither of them saw six zombies stumble out of a diner on the side of the street opposite their position at the van.

"May as well fill it up while we're here," Bundy said.

Mead didn't relish the thought of another drink of fuel, but he knew Bundy was right. Five gallons would take them another hundred or hundred fifty miles, and then they'd have to do this all over again.

While they waited for the gas to empty into the tank, they both missed a preteen zombie exit the broken glass doors of a red brick middle school further up the street. The young girl wore a *Frozen* t-shirt and most of the skin from her eyes up was missing. More zombies followed her out of the building—single file like an undead fire drill.

Bundy was almost finished transferring the gas when the florist zombie moved into view. She grabbed Bundy's arm, and he dropped the can. The remaining gasoline splashed over his feet.

"Why, you old hag," he said in the same matter-of-fact tone that frustrated Mead to no end.

Bundy pulled his arm free and grabbed a handful of her gray hair. He slammed her face into the side of the van, and the men could hear bones breaking. He smashed her another time for good measure, and she went limp.

He dropped her to the ground, and she fell on top of the gas can. Bundy bent down and rolled her off, then grabbed the container. When he stood up, he stared past Mead and realized the two zombies that had been roaming harmlessly upon their arrival were now within a few yards. He shoved the can at Mead and moved toward the front of the van, where the rifle was still propped on the hood.

Mead turned to follow the action and saw the zombies. He grabbed one of his sticks from the van. "I got thi—" He stopped when he saw the two zombies closing in from the front were now flanked by six zombies from the diner. "Fuck."

Bundy waved at him to circle around. "I'll get the two up front. You take the ones coming from the side."

Mead raised his stick, ready to dish out death, but before that happened, he saw the zombies from the school ambling up the street. There were too many to count. Over seventy. Maybe more than a hundred.

"Fuck," he said again. It was the only word that came to mind. It was all that needed to be said.

Bundy followed his gaze and saw the dozens of zombies marching toward them. Most looked to be young teens, many already sporting braces or marred by garish, purple pimples decorating their faces. Several adults, who had likely been teachers or administrators, mixed into the crowd. Some had obviously been attacked, with gaping bloody wounds that had long since stopped bleeding as evidence.

Bundy fired a bullet through the head of one of the zombies approaching from the front. Mead used his stick to impale one of his group through the ear, then swung around and chopped off the head of another. The school of zombies was within ten yards.

"We have to go! Get in the van!" Mead yelled.

Bundy saw more zombies coming in from the front. Three dozen, maybe four. "There are too many to drive through. We need to wait it out somewhere."

Mead dropped three more zombies with the stick, then searched around for an escape route. Zombies surrounded them, and they moved closer with every second that passed. I'm not going to die this soon, he thought. No way. It's not fair.

When he'd expressed that sentiment growing up, Mead's dad had always told him (usually along with a slap upside his head) that life wasn't fair, and it certainly wasn't. If it were, he wouldn't have been fathered by an illiterate, alcoholic dipshit who couldn't even hold onto his job burning up trash at the local dump. And his mother wouldn't have been a fifteen-year-old bimbo whose number one goal in life was getting social security disability. Life wasn't fair, but Mead wasn't ready for his to end yet.

He spotted a narrow fire escape staircase leading to the roof of a building across from the van.

"Over there!" Mead said as he ran for the stairs. He sliced open the stomach of a zombie that he passed along the way, and its rotten guts fell out in one big clump.

"They'll follow us!" Bundy yelled, but he chased Mead anyway. Running was not one of his regular pastimes, and he was out of breath within five thundering steps.

"Zombies can't climb steps."

Bundy struggled to keep up. He could hear the creatures closing in. "Are you sure?"

"Ninety-nine percent."

Mead hit the first step and looked back to see Bundy trailing by several yards. A dozen zombies were on his heels, and his inner monologue told him to leave the big man behind and climb. Instead, he ran back to Bundy. "Hustle, you fat fucker!"

Mead dropped the three zombies that were closest to the big man, then grabbed Bundy's arm and dragged him toward the staircase. When they got there, Mead pushed him forward, and the fat giant trudged up the steps as fast as possible, which was not fast at all.

Mead went up backward. He killed five more zombies that crowded the base of the steps. More were coming, but they were several yards away, so he turned forward. Bundy had only ascended eight steps. Mead shoved his hands into the man's ample soft ass and pushed him forward.

They made it to the top, both of them panting and exhausted.

"Thanks," was all Bundy could get out.

"Don't mention it."

They gazed over the rooftop. Hundreds of zombies filled the streets and the area around the van. Many of them moved toward the fire escape. Several were already there.

"If we stay up here and keep quiet, I think they'll forget about us pretty quick," Bundy said.

Mead was about to agree when a zombie climbed the first step. Then the second.

"Fuck." That perfect word again.

The zombie moved awkwardly, like a man with two new prosthetic legs, but it continued its upward trek.

Bundy looked at Mead, his face red with exhaustion or anger or both. "I thought you said they couldn't climb stairs."

Mead watched the zombie continue toward them, his lips turned downward in a petulant scowl. A second zombie started up the stairs, then a third. "I didn't think they could."

Bundy checked the access door on the roof and found it locked. He stared down at the street where the zombies teemed like ants at the base of their hill. Then he looked at the van and sighed heavily. "This really grinds my gears."

Mead turned to him. "What?"

Bundy shrugged the rifle strap off his shoulder and got into a shooter's stance. He aimed the barrel at the rear side window of the van. "Do you know what tannerite is?"

Mead shook his head. "No."

"Then duck down and cover your head."

Mead didn't understand what was happening, but he did as told. He stared at his feet and heard Bundy mutter, "Damned waste, this is."

As soon as those words were spoken, an explosion louder than anything Mead had ever heard shook the building that they were standing atop. Bundy fell on him, covering Mead with a quarter ton of sweaty flesh.

All he could hear was a constant ringing in his ears. He spotted something that looked like a burning black comet crash on the far side of the building and smash through the rooftop. Smaller objects followed. After ten seconds, the rain of fire ceased. After thirty, he could hear other sounds mixed in with the ringing.

"Are you all right?" Bundy asked as he crawled off him.

Mead was plastered flat against the roof. Bundy grabbed onto him with his oven mitt hand and roughly hoisted him to his feet.

"What? What the fuck happened?"

Bundy was looking over the edge of the roof, and Mead followed his gaze. The van was gone. The zombies were gone. All the buildings around them were charred and several were on fire.

"What the fuck?" Mead asked again.

Bundy sat on the squat, upraised barrier that framed in the roof. "Tannerite. About fifty pounds of it." That meant nothing to Mead, and Bundy, who was visibly annoyed, continued on.

"It's a powder that's used to make exploding shooting targets so you don't have to walk all the way down the range to see if you hit the bull's eye. I premixed all I had before I hit the road. Thought it might come in handy, but not like this."

Mead stared at the scorched wasteland below them. "Where's the van?"

Bundy pointed away from the road, toward the roof, where a chunk of metal smoked. "That looks like a quarter panel to me."

"You blew up the van?"

Bundy sneered, and Mead thought he might hit him, but he composed himself. "You didn't offer any better suggestions, asshole."

Mead remained quiet. That seemed the wisest choice.

"Now, we're minus one van plus all of my ammunition and guns, except this one." Bundy looked at the rifle, then to Mead as if he might use it on him. Instead, he walked to a dark hunk of debris, which had landed on the roof, picked it up, and examined it. "Huh. A foot." He tossed it over the edge, where it bounced against the blackened sidewalk.

"Ladders," Mead said.

Bundy looked at him, curious. "What?"

"It's ladders that zombies can't climb. Not stairs."

"Oh. Well, I suppose that's good to know."

CHAPTER TWENTY-TWO

It had been two days since the zombies overtook the bunker. Mitch had eaten nothing since the day he arrived, and his stomach felt like a balled-up fist inside his abdomen. A hungry fist. He wanted to search for food, but abandoning the safety of the control room was a fool's errand, and Mitch was no fool.

He stared at the wall of closed circuit TVs, which still had power thanks to the emergency generator. He was sure everyone out there was dead, or undead, depending on your point of view, but that didn't bother him half as much as the hunger pain gnawing away at his insides.

After abandoning his father, they fled E Wing and avoided the zombies, which were too busy eating fat cat Senators and Representatives. They're too lazy to run for anything other than office, Mitch thought.

Once free from the wing, they reached a long corridor, which, as Mitch knew from his studies, would lead them toward the front point of the triangular-shaped bunker. There, they'd come to the blast doors that opened to the hotel and, presumably, safety.

Before they reached the front of the bunker, they stumbled on a group of soldiers who had turned. There were eight of them. Three looked intact, but the other five had various bites and chunks taken out of them, probably from each other.

Now, they were a unified squad, and when they saw Mitch and Margaret, they took off like hounds after foxes. Son and mother zigged and zagged through the mazes of hallways and rooms, and Mitch lost his bearings.

As they rounded a corner, Mitch hit a wet spot on the floor and went flying. He came to rest against the wall, and Margaret dashed to his side. As he crawled onto his knees, he saw what had caused him to fall. A pile of guts the size of a bushel basket sat on the tile floor like a jellyfish bobbing on the ocean.

"Are you hurt?" Margaret asked.

As Mitch climbed to his feet, his gore-soaked sneakers made it feel like he was standing on an oil slick. "I'm fine. We have to keep going."

He led her forward, but less than a dozen yards later, they came across an old man who lurched toward them like Frankenstein.

"Oh, my God. That's Frank Sandoval," Margaret said.

Mitch never shared his father's interest in politics, but the name rang a bell, and he thought Sandoval was either Secretary of State or Defense. He never quite understood the difference anyway.

He saw the Secretary's white dress shirt had turned red at the bottom, and when he walked, it floated back and forth, revealing a hollow cavern where his insides had been. So, you're the son of a bitch who left his guts all over the floor, Mitch thought.

Mitch saw a fire ax framed on the wall like a shadowbox. He smacked his elbow against the pane. It shattered, dropping shards of glass to the floor. The sound made the Secretary pick up his pace, and Mitch could hear him growling. Actually growling, like a fucking dog.

Mitch grabbed the ax from its perch and turned back to Sandoval. "I really liked these shoes."

The Secretary growled again, and Mitch ran at him. They met

like jousters, but Mitch was the only one with a weapon, and he slammed the ax into Sandoval's face.

It hit just below his nose, and the blade chopped through the zombie's upper jaw with a heavy crunch that Mitch felt reverberate all the way down to his feet. It didn't cut the whole way through, but it did the job, and the zombie collapsed in a heap on the floor.

Behind them, Margaret wailed like a siren. Mitch let go of the ax handle and ran to her. "Quiet!" She kept screaming. "Shut up, or you'll draw all of them to us!"

She was too wound up to stop all at once, and the shriek tapered off like someone slowly turning down the volume on the stereo. But it was too late.

The eight soldier zombies rushed onto the scene. They were quickly joined by more than a dozen others. Then several dozen more. Mitch grabbed Margaret's wrist and pulled her in the opposite direction. They ran as fast as they could for as long as they could, and when Margaret tired, Mitch dragged her.

They came upon the control room by accident. Through large glass windows, Mitch spotted a man wearing oversized headphones that looked like earmuffs. His back was turned toward them.

Margaret bent at the waist, coughing and wheezing. Mitch wanted to tell her again to shut up, but he knew it would be a waste. Instead, he rapped his knuckles against the glass to get the man's attention.

"Hey! Let us in!"

He didn't react at first, so Mitch hit the glass again, harder this time. The man swiveled the chair around. By the time it made it ninety degrees, Mitch was pretty sure he was dead. At a hundred twenty, he was positive.

The zombie's lifeless eyes stared ahead, blank and seeing at the same time. When he saw Mitch and his mother, his lips peeled back in a sneer, revealing brown, coffee-stained teeth.

Mitch heard Margaret start to cry again, but over her soft whimpers, he heard footsteps. It sounded like hundreds of them, all moving in their direction. Fast. He looked to his mother, and her blank, shell-shocked expression revealed that she was of no help.

The footsteps closed in. There were so many Mitch thought he could feel the concrete floor vibrating through the soles of his bloodied sneakers. He looked toward the green light spilling from the corridor. It was only seconds before black shadows invaded that glow. And behind the shadows were a legion of zombies.

Mitch grabbed his mother's limp wrist and pulled her toward the control room. She followed behind, lost in a fog. Mitch took the key card from his pocket. He had no idea whether or not it would work, but as he glanced back and saw hundreds of zombies pouring out of the hall and racing at them, he knew it was their only chance.

He swiped the card. The light flipped green, and the door clicked. Mitch threw it open and dashed inside. He jerked Margaret in with him, and she tumbled to the floor in a daze. Mitch grabbed hold of the door and pushed to close it. Before it could latch, a woman in a power suit, who was missing all the flesh on her neck, shoved her arm through the opening.

Mitch slammed the door, pinning her arm. She didn't even flinch when her skin tore. Mitch opened it a few inches and slammed it again. That time, her flesh split to the bone, but she insisted on pressing forward, and Mitch could feel his strength fading.

He grabbed her forearm and jerked it backward, using the door as a fulcrum. He heard it snap, and the sound gave him another burst of adrenaline. He launched his shoulder against the door. It closed. Her severed arm flopped onto the floor at Mitch's feet, and he watched the hand contract and twitch once, then twice, before stopping.

As soon as the door closed, more zombies pounded against it, but the heavy steel held tough. Mitch turned his back to it and realized he was completely out of breath. He steadied himself, but as soon as he thought it was time for a break, he saw that his mother was going to die.

Margaret stared out the reinforced glass windows, mesmerized by the hundreds of zombies desperately trying to get in. She was unaware of the one already amongst them. The man who had once manned the control center staggered toward her and was only two awkward steps away.

Mitch ran across the room as fast as his exhausted legs could carry him.

"Watch out!" he screamed the words, but Margaret barely reacted. She was neck-deep in shock and clueless.

Mitch was a yard away, but the zombie was closer. It leaned in, bared its baby shit brown teeth, and bit into Margaret's lily white shoulder. Her eyes flared, suddenly alert, and that made it worse.

The zombie ripped back its head and took with it a mouthful of Margaret's flesh. Mitch pushed his mother aside and rammed his shoulder into the chest of the much taller ghoul.

The zombie stumbled backward and tripped over its own swivel chair before hitting the floor. Mitch looked around the room. Why hadn't he dug the ax out of the Secretary's head?

On a cluttered desk, his eyes fell upon a fancy letter opener designed to look like a miniature sword. He grabbed it. The blade was six inches long.

The zombie was on its knees and working its way back to its feet. When Mitch stepped in front of it, the zombie stared forward and growled. Mitch gripped the letter opener in his fist and stabbed hard.

The tip of the blade struck the zombie in the temple, and Mitch was surprised when he felt a brief pop, like cracking a peanut shell, and the blade continued inward until it was buried to the quillon. The monster tumbled face first onto the concrete floor. Mitch pulled out the letter opener and gave the zombie a kick, just to make sure it was dead. It was.

Mitch turned away from it and looked to his mother, who stood in the exact same spot, holding her shoulder. Blood gushed from the shredded wound, and the left side of her body had gone red. She looked at her son, her eyes full of tears and pain and fear.

"He bit me, Mitch. He got me good. What do you think's going to happen?"

Mitch stepped to her. She looked so pitiful standing there, her sanity on a precipice and covered in her own blood. He reached out and held her hand.

"You'll be okay, Mom."

"Are you sure? There's a lot of blood."

"Let me see."

She turned robotically away from him. He saw the wound was deep, but the blood flow had slowed to a bare trickle. And it was crazy, but he thought the flesh around the bite already looked dark and decayed. He put his hand on her shoulder reassuringly.

"The bleeding's already stopped."

"So, I'll be all right?" The hopefulness in her voice made Mitch want to puke.

"You'll be fine."

"That's good. Because I'm not ready to leave you, Mitch. I love you too much."

"I love you, too, Mom."

Mitch slid the blade into the small indentation where the base of the skull met the top of her neck. She inhaled sharply, her breathing sounding like a whistle. There was a soft "Uh," and then she went limp. Mitch caught her under the arms before she fell, then eased her to the floor.

CHAPTER TWENTY-THREE

ABEN HAD BEEN WALKING ALONG AN OAK TREE-LINED TWO-LANE road when he heard the car approaching from the east. He estimated it to be a mile away. Maybe two. Noise traveled far in this quiet, dead world.

He had enough time to drag a medium-sized tree branch across the road, move into the cover of the trees, and wait. The dog had been trailing behind him all morning, and he saw it watching from about ten yards away.

"Get back. Just until we see who's coming."

As if understanding Aben's words, the dog crawled under a tangle of mountain laurel and laid down. They waited.

The car came into view and slowed as it approached the branch. Aben watched as the passenger side door opened and a man sporting a military haircut stepped out. Aben noticed the man had an AK rifle slung over his shoulder.

"Hell, we could've drove right over this!" the man hollered to the driver as he dragged the branch off the road and tossed it into the vegetation.

Aben tried to see the driver, but couldn't make him out through the sunlight reflecting off the windows. He did, however, hear his voice. "It's not worth risking a flat."

The gray-haired man started back to the car and Aben knew he had only seconds to decide whether to make his presence known or not. As the man reclaimed his position in the shotgun seat, Aben rolled the proverbial dice.

"Hey, there."

The older man's head snapped around and his hands went quickly and instinctively toward his rifle. In one smooth move, it was raised and ready to fire. He was former military, that was certain, and Aben hoped Father Time had slowed his trigger finger.

"I'm coming out and I'd appreciate it if you don't shoot me."

As Aben moved clear of the tree line, he heard a second set of footsteps on the pavement. And hushed voices.

"I've got us covered, Bol," the same gruff voice of the man who'd moved the branch said.

"God, just don't shoot anyone."

"Can never be too careful."

Aben liked the second voice better. There was a calmness in the words and the tone. It lacked the anxious and eager timbre of the rifle-holder.

When Aben stepped into the clear, he was shocked to discover the driver was the younger of the two. He was dark haired and square-jawed and stood with the kind of posture that gets beaten into you during boot camp. The kind you never lose.

Aben held his hand and stump up as he approached them. "I don't mean any harm. I can promise you that."

The older man still had him lined up, even though he was less than ten yards away. The younger placed his hand on the rifle barrel and forced it down.

"Enough, Dash. We've been hoping to find someone who was still alive. Now that we found one, let's not kill him."

Dash returned the rifle to its previous resting place on his shoulder, but still appeared wary.

"I'm Jorge Bolivar. That's Ted Dash."

"Aben." He extended his hand and Bolivar shook it. When he did, Bolivar's attention was on Aben's stump.

"You all right there?"

Aben glanced at it. The bandage was the shit brown color of dried blood. He'd been meaning to change it, but hadn't gotten around to it. "Oh, it hasn't rotted off yet, so I suppose it's just fine."

"I'm a medic. I'm happy to take a look, just in case."

Aben nodded. "I'd appreciate that."

They sat at the side of the road while Bolivar examined Aben's stump.

"It sure won't be pretty, but there's no infection. Keep it clean and you should be fine."

While Bolivar cleaned the wound, Aben shared bits of how he lost his appendage and the other men told him of the downfall of D.C. and their journeys thus far.

Aben thought Dash might be crazy, but he'd met plenty of crazy men during his years in the Marines and wasn't put off by that. The older man seemed to accept him into their small cadre and Aben felt comfortable enough to whistle for the dog. It came without hesitation.

"I'll be," Bolivar said. "I thought that plague took out all the dogs, too."

"This is the only one I've seen. Don't think they fared much better than us."

The mutt crawled onto Bol's lap and licked his face. The man laughed and scratched its ears.

"Mind his leg."

"Have you seen anyone else alive?" Bolivar asked Aben.

Aben shook his head. "No. You boys are the first, I'm afraid. But I haven't put on nearly as many miles as you."

"Why didn't you boost a ride?" Dash asked.

"I prefer to walk." He left it at that. Even though these other men were both soldiers and likely had similar tales of their own, his story was one he didn't care to reminisce upon, let alone share out loud.

Bolivar examined the dog's leg and gave it the all clear. They would both live. For now.

"There's room in the car for you and the pooch, if you're interested," Bol said.

"I might be. What do you have planned?"

As Bolivar and Dash told Aben about the plan to seek out the bunker, Aben thought the idea to be one of the stupidest he'd ever heard, but he managed to keep his opinion to himself. He was proud of that. Maybe he wasn't hopeless after all. When the car hit the road, both he and the dog were along for the ride.

CHAPTER TWENTY-FOUR

JULI WAS DOING FIFTY MILES PER HOUR WHEN JEREMY TURNED. He'd been silent as night turned to morning and Helen had even taken a break from worrying about him to fall asleep.

The old woman's head was careened back against the seat and her mouth hung agape as deep, raspy snores rumbled from her throat. Juli smiled a little, remembering how Mark used to snore when he slept, but the smile faded when that memory was swiftly replaced with the one of killing him.

They'd cleared the city some time ago, but Juli could still see hints of smoke in the sky behind her as she drove. It was a nice enough day otherwise. The weather was warm and spring-like. If she hadn't been running for her life, she might have been outside, planting petunias and impatiens, digging her hands through the soft potting soil as the chickadees serenaded her.

The realization that she'd probably never do any of those things again made the beautiful, blue sky seem pointless. What had Helen said? The end of days?

Maybe she was right. Maybe the world wasn't going to end in an ice age or fireballs from the sky after all. Maybe this was it. She'd never been a philosopher, and she had little time to ponder the end of the world because Helen's snores were replaced with screams.

Juli checked the rearview mirror and saw Jeremy gnawing away at his grandmother's bony shoulder.

"Stop it, Jeremy! Stop!" Helen flailed with her stick-thin arms, pounding her fists into the boy, but he wouldn't stop eating.

"Get off her!" Julie screamed as she slammed on the brakes. The duo in the back vaulted forward, crashing into the front seats. That broke them apart, and Helen scrambled across the seat and away from the boy.

His mouth was stained with his grandmother's blood, and he struggled to climb free from the footwell. Juli realized she had to stop that and jumped out of the car.

"Stay away from him, Helen!" Juli threw open the rear passenger side door and grabbed the boy by his hair.

Jeremy snarled and swung at her, but Juli refused to let go as she dragged him out of the vehicle. Still holding two fistfuls of hair, she slammed his face against the ground once, then a second time.

The boy's movements slowed but didn't stop. Juli smashed his face against the roadway a third time and felt a crunch. He went limp.

Juli knelt over his lifeless body, catching her breath. She realized she was still holding onto him and quickly let go. A few wiry, black hairs remained stuck to her sweaty hands.

I just killed him, she thought. I killed this boy right in front of his grandmother. She wiped her hands on her nightgown to free herself of his hair. As she was doing so, ninety pounds of force landed on her back, and she crumpled forward against Jeremy's body.

Helen was atop her. The newly undead woman felt like fire on Juli's back. She clawed and scratched, and only Juli's nightgown prevented her skin from being shredded.

The dead woman grabbed Juli's arm. She was so strong that it felt like she could tear it right off her body. I'm going to die, Juli thought.

The realization didn't upset her. She'd been in a fog since seeing her dead daughter, killing her husband, and discovering her son had become a zombie. That was a three-course meal from which she'd never recover. Her life was already over. This was just paying the check.

Pinned between the two people she'd tried to save the night before, Juli waited to die. As Helen's thick saliva dripped onto the nape of her neck, it dawned on her that she didn't want to die after all.

Juli threw her head backward and felt a jarring collision as her skull collided with Helen's face. Tiny stars appeared before her eyes.

Helen's frantic clawing and scratching stopped for a moment, and Juli she felt the weight atop her shift. The reprieve was only long enough for Juli to roll onto her side. When she looked up, she saw blood running out of Helen's broken nose.

When Juli moved, Helen's focus returned to her. Juli grabbed Helen's shirt and pushed the zombie backward. Helen swung and flailed at her, her brittle nails drawing blood.

Juli caught Helen's arm and pulled her in close. They were face to face. When Juli stared into Helen's red, crazed eyes, she knew it was now or never.

Juli twisted her head and lunged for the old woman's neck. She bit down on Helen's throat and felt the flesh give way.

Hot blood gushed into Juli's mouth, but she kept biting until her teeth caught what felt like a thick string of gristle. She bit harder, and that, too, gave way. Now, the blood was spraying, pumping out of the zombie and into Juli's face.

Helen grabbed for her throat, and Juli rolled, which knocked Helen off her and onto the road. Juli darted back to the Audi and dove into the driver's seat.

She'd left the engine running, and she threw the SUV into reverse, cranked the wheel hard to the right, and watched in the mirror as the rear end of the car slammed into Helen. The back end bucked and bounced as it rolled over her, then the front wheels did a repeat.

Through the windshield, Juli could now see the zombie's twisted, mangled corpse sprawled on the highway. Then, Helen tried to get up. Juli waited until the zombie was on its knees, which put its head right at bumper level. She shifted into drive and slammed the gas.

Juli felt a heavy thud as the vehicle plowed into the woman. She kept driving and didn't look back.

Juli's mouth was filled with the taste of blood, and she spat twice into the passenger seat to rid herself of the flavor. That only half worked.

She caught her reflection in the mirror and saw that Helen's blood drenched her upper body. She felt nauseous, but that was mostly the lingering flavor of the blood in her mouth.

She wasn't horrified at what she'd just done; she felt accomplished. Before this, Juli had assumed her life was over. Now, she thought she might have some living to do after all. But first, she wanted some new clothing. And a cigarette.

CHAPTER TWENTY-FIVE

MEAD SAW THE AMBULANCE FIRST. HE DROVE A BMW SUV they'd found shortly after blowing up half the town. Bundy's explosion trick was a good one and had killed every single zombie that had them trapped. But, as the big man had lamented, it had also wiped out their weaponry.

All they'd escaped with was Mead's trusty hockey stick and Bundy's rifle. That didn't bother Mead tremendously because he knew he could fend for himself. Bundy, on the other hand, was fucked without his guns. More proof guns are a bad option in a zombie apocalypse, Mead thought.

The big red bus sat in the middle of the interstate, and Mead wasn't sure it was real at first. It could've been a hazy mirage in the heat brought on by tired eyes and the hypnosis that goes along with highway driving. But as they neared it, it became clear that the ambulance was very real.

The front end faced away from them, which prevented Mead from seeing inside, but he assumed that if there were any occupants, they were dead.

A line from an old zombie movie about sending more paramedics came to mind, and Mead started laughing and couldn't stop.

His shrill giggles woke Bundy, who hadn't stopped being butt hurt over the stairs fiasco. Mead liked him better when he was sleeping.

"What's so damn funny?" Bundy asked.

Bundy had been irritated ever since the rooftop incident, and it was wearing on Mead's psyche. He kept trying to impress the man, to keep the mood upbeat, but it was growing harder by the hour.

"Nothing. There's an ambulance ahead," Mead said.

Bundy sat forward in his seat and rubbed his sleepy eyes. "Pull over."

Mead did, slowing the BMW to a stop at the back corner of the ambulance. He left the engine running as he jumped out and grabbed his hockey stick. Bundy followed, slowly.

When Mead moved beside the ambulance, he heard something thump against the side wall. He jumped back a step, then hopped onto the side rail and got eye level with the driver's side window. From there, he saw the woman.

She was bone skinny and motionless. He thought she might be dead, but he couldn't see any wounds on her, and so far, he hadn't seen zombies sleep. It was a quandary.

He glanced back at Bundy. "There's a woman inside."

"Dead?"

Mead shrugged his shoulders. "Can't tell." He pulled up on the door handle and found it locked. "It's locked."

"I assumed as much when it didn't open."

That rotten attitude again. Mead didn't bother responding. He rapped the end of the hockey stick against the window and waited. She gave no response. "Pretty sure she's dead."

Another loud thud rocked the ambulance.

"Whatever's back here sure isn't," Bundy said.

"Try the back door."

BUNDY MOVED to the rear doors. He'd grown to highly dislike the little man who now watched him with the hungry, excited eyes of an animal. Part of it, a big part, was because he blamed Mead for losing his collection of firearms. But it was more than that. The dude annoyed him on general principle. He was anxious and shifty. Mead was exhausting to be around.

Bundy would have dropped him a few hundred miles ago if the kid hadn't been such a good fighter. In Bundy's thick, bear paw hands, that goofy-looking hockey stick was useless, but Mead handled it like an actual ninja, and he'd destroyed a shocking number of zombies without so much as firing a single bullet.

The kid was wired on energy drinks, and Bundy slept while Mead drove straight through the night. Bundy had woken up when the morning light penetrated his still closed eyelids, and he faked it for a while, hoping to avoid Mead's incessant chatter. He'd have continued to feign sleep if it hadn't been for the ambulance.

This is where we'll split up, Bundy thought. I'll take the bus, he can have the Beemer. Sayonara, you odd, little man. He kept his finger on the trigger of his sole remaining rifle as he reached for the door handle and eased it open.

The first thing he saw was chaos. It looked as if the entire contents of the ambulance had been knocked to the floor and repeatedly beaten and smashed.

Amidst the destruction, he saw the zombie. Bits of glass and shards of debris covered its dark blue paramedic uniform. As his gaze carried up to its face, Bundy saw two syringes jutting from its eye sockets. Red gore had trickled down its cheeks and dried, bloody tears leaking from the black holes where its eyes had once been.

"Son of a bitch." The words came out in an exhale, and when they did, the zombie turned toward him like a weather vane in a strong wind. It stumbled at him, tripping over the wreckage under its feet, which suddenly made more sense to Bundy.

He took a few steps back from the ambulance and watched as the zombie climbed back to its feet, fell again, then resorted to crawling on all fours toward him.

When it reached the back of the bus, its feeling hands hit the open air. It fell ass over head out the doorway and landed face first on the road. Bundy winced as the fall drove the syringes deeper into its eye sockets.

"What's going on?" Mead called out.

Bundy didn't answer. He was enjoying the show. The zombie pushed itself back onto its knees, then got to its feet. Its arms flailed wildly, desperate for a target. Bundy kept backing away, staying just out of reach.

He didn't see Mead jogging onto the scene until he was just a few feet away with the stick raised. Not this time, slick. This one's mine.

Bundy hurriedly shouldered the rifle, aimed, and fired. The bullet ripped through the blind zombie's face, smashing out its front teeth, then exploding the back of its skull in a spray of red. The spent bullet whizzed just a few feet by Mead and embedded itself in the side of the ambulance.

Mead jumped back and dropped his stick, which clattered against the concrete. "What the fuck!"

Bundy lowered the rifle slowly, deliberately. "Didn't see you." His voice was not apologetic.

Mead's eyes blazed, but he didn't respond. He pushed his greasy hair out of his face and bent to pick up the stick. When he stood, the woman spoke.

"Who are you?"

Both men looked to Mina, who stood beside the driver's door of the ambulance. She stared at them, curious and wary.

"I thought you were dead. You looked it," Mead said.

"You were wrong. And you didn't answer me."

Bundy strode toward her, grinning over her thinly veiled annoyance with Mead. "I'm Bundy."

"Like the wrestler or the serial killer?"

"Like neither. It's just a name."

Mina extended her bony hand, and when Bundy took it on his own, he thought it looked like a bird's foot laying in a catcher's mitt. "Mina Costell. Is your friend incapable of answering a simple question?"

Mead didn't bother with a handshake. "Mead."

Mina looked past them, toward the dead zombie on the road. "I was calling him Ray. As in Charles."

"Were you the one that blinded it?" Bundy asked.

She nodded. "He's been with me for a few hundred miles."

"Why didn't you kill it?" Mead's voice was an amalgamation of contempt and confusion.

"He was company, of sorts."

As Mead stomped back to the BMW, Bundy and Mina exchanged a grin. "He's an intense one."

"You don't know the half of it," Bundy said. "But he's alive, and that seems pretty rare now."

He looked her up and down. She looked like a twig he could break in two, but he saw dried blood all over her. It was obvious that she was no helpless waif. "Want to make our duo a trio?"

Mina looked to Mead, who sulked behind the wheel of the Beemer, then back to the mountain that was Bundy. "I won't ride with two men I only just met, but I'll follow along a while."

Bundy liked the sound of that. "Get back in the ambulance, and we'll lead the way."

Mina nodded and gave his bicep, which was bigger than her waist, a short caress. "Good."

CHAPTER TWENTY-SIX

"It's called a *Rattenkönig*. I saw a mummified version in a German science museum," Emory said.

"There were upwards of two dozen rats knotted together. It was rather horrifying. If memory serves, they were first discovered just before the bubonic plague in the 1300s wiped out a third of the world's population."

Wim thought about that for a good while.

After the incident on the highway, the two men had agreed to pack it in for the day. A roadside motel which the sign out front declared, "Yellow Hat Motor Court," seemed empty enough. Neither had any qualms about taking a key from the pegboard behind the desk without paying.

"Let's go with three. It's my lucky number," Emory had said. The motel was free of travelers and zombies, and that, coupled with twin beds, was all they needed.

Wim had told Emory about the abomination of rats he'd found in the barn in the days preceding the outbreak, and as he told the tale, the old man's eyes brightened. "They called it a Rat King."

That seemed fitting to Wim. But having a name to put with the thing he'd seen and destroyed did little to allay the unease of Emory's comments about the plague's effect on the population. "What percentage of people would you suppose have been killed by this?"

Emory mulled it over. "I've been thinking about that a lot the last few days. You're the only other non-infected person I've met, and... Now, I don't mean to alarm you..."

"Be candid. The time for coddling is long past."

"Well, there is simply no way to know if we are immune or if there's the equivalent of a ticking time bomb inside us. There's a real possibility that this disease has simply decided to take a few days or weeks longer than the typical incubation period before it explodes."

Wim watched him for a moment, then smirked. "That's interesting, but you didn't answer my question."

"Oh, yes. About the mortality rate. Well..." He broke eye contact with Wim, and Wim noticed. He also noticed the deep wrinkles that etched the old man's face were even darker than normal—black gashes across his forehead and under his eyes. "It's impossible to say. There are too many uncertainties."

"But you have an idea."

Emory looked back at him and nodded. "I do. If what I've seen, and what you've told me, holds true elsewhere... It's considerably higher than ninety-nine percent."

He folded his hands, his fingers stiff and the knuckles fat with rheumatism. "Frankly, I'd be shocked if more than one person in ten thousand survived the virus, or whatever it was.

"And when you factor in the people who were killed by the... zombies, I guess we're calling them that. Or the people who perished from heart attacks due to the stress like I almost did, or had an asthma attack and couldn't go to the pharmacy for a new inhaler, or small children who have no one to care for them..."

His shoulders sagged. "It could very easily be one in a hundred thousand. Maybe even one in a million, Wim."

Wim sighed heavily. He appreciated Emory's candor, and deep

down—he'd had the same thoughts—but hearing it said aloud carried a gravitas that felt uncomfortably real. "Like hitting the lottery."

Emory smiled a bit when Wim said that, and some of the darkness and worry fled his face. "I suppose so. That would make us winners, would it not?"

Wim didn't feel like a winner, but he liked seeing the old man smile. Emory had told him bits of his life's story since they met, and although the two couldn't be more opposite, Wim felt an admiration so strong that it bordered on infatuation.

He loved listening as Emory discussed backpacking through Europe or driving a Land Rover across the Australian Outback. And even though Emory was the first gay man Wim had met in his entire life, when he talked about his early years with his partner, the age melted off him like snow on a tin roof. Wim found himself so envious of experiencing that kind of love that he felt a physical ache deep inside himself.

"Have you ever loved someone, Wim? Someone other than family?"

"No, Sir." It seemed like there should be more to add. An excuse as to why a thirty-two-year-old man was so inexperienced in many ways, but he couldn't find the words. Probably because there weren't any to find.

"I view love as life's greatest blessing and its most devious curse. The person you love occupies your thoughts every waking moment. They're with you all day long, whether in physical form or not. You fall asleep thinking about them, and then you dream about them. In the morning, the whole show starts over again."

"So, why's that bad?"

"Because love isn't always reciprocated. Actually, I'd say it seldom is, at least in equal parts. One person always loves a little harder. Needs a little more. It's like an old-fashioned money scale." Emory held his hands up at an even level, then lowered one while raising the other. "And when that happens, the balance gets lost. One side keeps falling further and further behind the other, and, eventually, it's passed the tipping point, and it bottoms out."

"Which one were you?"

Emory flashed a smirk that could have been rueful, but light flickered in his eyes. "Grant wanted to love me. In fact, he did at first; I'm certain of it. Maybe even up until the bitter end. But Grant had a veneer that I never managed to penetrate. Perhaps it was there to protect himself, but it was always a barrier between us."

"Did you ever think about divorce? Or, I guess it would have been a separation."

"Not for a nanosecond. He was the love of my life, even if he couldn't reciprocate in the way I would have wished. And I loved him for his so-called faults, not in spite of them. He challenged me in a way no one else ever did." His eyes drifted away from Wim's gaze.

"Even in the later years, when it seemed like we were virtual strangers in that big house, I'd still wake eager to see him. I'd go to Grant's quarters. We had separate bedrooms for decades. I'd stand in the doorway and watch him. Sometimes, only for a few seconds. Sometimes, so long that my knees would get sore and my back stiff.

“And his face, so peaceful and soft as he slept, was the face of the man I saw dancing across that stage decades earlier. It didn't matter that his hair had gone gray or his skin was as wrinkled as a newspaper that had been crumpled into a ball and flattened back out again.

"I always fled before he woke, but even during the darkest years, I gazed at him on those mornings and found peace. And in many ways, that's even better than love."

It was so dark inside the room the two could barely see each other, but when Wim felt a yawn coming on, he covered his mouth to hide it.

"I'm tired, too," Emory said.

"It's been a long day."

"Indeed it has. And we've earned a good night's sleep."

Emory was asleep when his head hit the pillow. Wim lasted

slightly longer. He watched the stars outside the motel room window. Billions of stars.

There used to be billions of us, too. He tried to imagine the sky if 99.9999% of the stars winked out. The idea that there might only be a few thousand people left alive in the whole, entire world dominated his thoughts until he drifted off.

When he woke the next morning and found the motel surrounded by zombies, he realized he'd left all the guns in the Bronco. It was a stupid mistake, and in this new world, stupid mistakes got you killed.

He felt bad that Emory was going to die for his carelessness. And he regretted that he'd never get to see Ramey again. But most of all, he wished God would have spared someone smarter and more deserving of that one-in-a-million winning lottery ticket that he'd just wasted.

CHAPTER TWENTY-SEVEN

RAMEY NEARED A SCHOOL BUS THAT SAT DISABLED AT THE SIDE of the road, felled by a flat tire. She slowed the truck as she passed and peered into the windows. Most were blood-stained, and some cracked.

She caught motion inside, figures roaming through the confines of the bus. When she got to the front, she saw eight dead children pawing at the windshield, trying to escape. Their small, undead faces gave her goosebumps, and the site had her on edge for the next half hour.

As she rounded a sharp, downward sloping curve, she saw two figures on the road ahead. She thought they were corpses, but when she got within twenty yards, she saw movement. Not just moving, fighting. Ramey closed the gap to ten yards. She rested her hand on top of the cold gun on the seat beside her and watched.

The two were almost perfect opposites. The one on top was young, tall, thin, and male. The woman on the bottom was older, short, and round. They made Ramey think of that old comedy act she sometimes watched on TV. Laurel and something. Harvey?

At first, she thought they were both alive, but she soon realized the boy's movements had the herky-jerky zombie mannerisms she'd seen so often. The woman was alive, and she was losing the fight.

Ramey opened her door and jumped down from the truck. She tried to line the sights up with the zombie's head, but it looked like a pinpoint. Every time she breathed, it dipped out of alignment.

You can do this, she thought. Just focus and aim. Focus and aim. She held her breath and pulled the trigger.

Ramey saw a spray of blood, and the zombie boy flinched backward and grabbed at his throat. A second later, he dove at the woman, who struggled to hold him back.

"Damn it!" Ramey aimed again. Fired. This time, the round slammed into the boy's shoulder and sent him teetering off-balance.

The woman pushed him the rest of the way over, and he hit the ground with a thud. She rolled out from under him and looked to Ramey as she staggered to her feet. She didn't see the boy stand up and run, but Ramey did.

Ramey leveled off the gun. The woman's eyes grew so wide Ramey could see white all around the iris.

"Don't! I'm normal!"

Ramey shot again and saw a red mist burst from the side of the zombie's head. He dropped in a heap. She hated that it had taken three bullets to get the job done, but better late than never. The woman whose life Ramey had saved looked behind her and saw the dead boy on the road.

"Holy shit! I thought you were gonna kill me! But thanks."

Ramey flicked the gun's safety on and tucked it into the side of her belt. "Of course."

"I'm Peggy Benoit."

Peggy extended a hand, and they shook. The woman's grip was strong as a man's, and Ramey was relieved when she let go.

Ramey guessed the woman to be in her mid-fifties. She had a bowl cut of black hair that had gone at least half gray. She wore no makeup, black trousers, and a blue work shirt. Ramey didn't know if she was a lesbian but thought she looked the part.

"Ramey." Ramey motioned to the dead boy on the ground. "Did you know him?"

Peggy nodded. "Teddy Stader. He's been riding my bus since kindergarten. A little weird, but a good kid."

"I passed a school bus a little while ago. That was yours?"

Peggy's eyes clouded over with tears, but she fought them back before they could take an escape route down her cheeks. "Yeah. It was..." She didn't finish. Instead, she looked at Ramey's truck, which still idled in the roadway. "Where are you going?"

"To West Virginia. To look for my father."

"You don't think he's alive, do you?"

Her bluntness didn't bother Ramey. It was a question she asked herself a hundred times an hour. "Not really. But I have to know for sure."

"Oh." Peggy's eyes narrowed, and it was clear that she thought the idea stupid.

Ramey knew she was being judged and wasn't a fan of it. She had just saved the woman's life, after all. "Do you have anyone?"

"No." Peggy tapped her foot in a rapid, nervous tic.

Ramey tried to think of something to say, but Peggy beat her to it.

"Could I go with you? If you don't mind." Her voice broke, and she looked at the ground. "I'd really like to go."

Ramey hadn't had the best luck with companions, but she couldn't leave anyone alone with no vehicle, no protection.

"Of course. We can even take turns driving, if you're up for it."

Peggy glanced up and half-smiled. "Been doing it for a living for thirty-four years. Think I could manage."

"Good." Ramey moved toward the truck, but Peggy lagged behind.

"Ramey?"

She looked back.

"Could we move him off the road first? We don't have to bury him or anything, but it don't feel right just letting him lay there like roadkill. And he saved my ass earlier. Kinda feel like I owe him."

Ramey looked at the dead boy and nodded. "Yeah. I'll help."

Together, they dragged the boy into a field of Kentucky bluegrass and clover. Peggy knelt down at his side and folded his hands over his chest, then tousled his hair, which had been cut into a mohawk and dyed green.

"I'm sorry, bud." Peggy stood up and nodded her head. "Let's go."

So they did.

CHAPTER TWENTY-EIGHT

MEAD SPIED THE WAREHOUSE FIRST. BUNDY WAS TOO BUSY staring out the window with stars in his eyes over the broad they'd met in the ambulance.

The steel-sided building was at least three hundred feet long and even wider. A large electronic billboard out front was blank, but a faded placard on the front wall read, "Gilbert Paving & Heavy Construction."

No cars occupied the parking lot, which Mead felt lowered the likelihood of zombies inside. He also saw plenty of doors, from regular entryways to huge garage bays. Another plus.

Mead wasn't a fan of taking shelter indoors because it was easy to become surrounded and trapped. This warehouse, however, seemed mostly immune from those issues.

"Check that out," he said to Bundy.

Bundy came out of his daydream and looked ahead. "What about it?"

"Might be a good place to rest and regroup."

Bundy shrugged his shoulders. "Maybe."

When they reached the long driveway heading to the warehouse, he turned in. The ambulance followed. After stopping at the entrance, Mead bounced out of the BMW, grabbing his stick on the way. Bundy also got out of the SUV but didn't follow. Mina strolled toward the big man.

"What are we doing here?"

Mead ignored them as he bounded to the front doors.

"Mead thought it would be a good place to rest up."

"He never heard of a hotel?"

Bitch. Mead pretended not to hear.

"His idea, not mine," Bundy said.

The door opened to reveal an industrial waiting area filled with metal and vinyl furniture, tables littered with magazines like *Popular Mechanics* and *Field & Stream*, and a healthy layer of dust on the tile floor.

It looked completely undisturbed, and while Mead knew that wasn't a guarantee, it was another good omen. He glanced toward the lot, where Bundy and Mina mulled.

"Looks empty," he called to them.

Mina huffed. "Is there a reason you want us to hole up inside some factory and not a house or a hotel?"

Mead wanted to respond sarcastically but stopped himself. He took a breath, then spoke. "Houses and hotels are more likely to have people. Dead people. And it's too easy to get trapped. This is safer. Besides, there might be cool shit inside."

Mina and Bundy exchanged a glance. Mead could tell they realized his points were valid. Why didn't people just trust him? He knew his shit. "I'll do a run-through and make sure it's clear if you want to bring whatever supplies we have left."

With that, he disappeared into the building.

"Doesn't he ever get tired?" Mina asked.

"Not to my knowledge. He's like that Energizer bunny. He just keeps going and going and going and—"

"I get it."

Mina took two small plastic bags of groceries she'd gathered during an earlier stop. Bundy took his rifle and a few more bags of food. Then they headed into the warehouse.

WHILE MEAD EXPLORED every nook and cranny of the warehouse, Mina followed Bundy through a few of the cavernous garage bays, which were filled with heavy equipment. Bundy pointed at a gigantic steam roller.

"What do you think? If we had that, we wouldn't need to drive around zombies. We could roll right over 'em."

Mina raised an eyebrow. Was he serious? "How fast does one of those go?"

"I don't know. Four miles an hour, maybe. Five."

"Oh, so we could make it to Florida in about two years."

He looked at her. "Is that where you're heading? Florida?"

Mina shrugged her shoulders. She hadn't given it much thought. "It's warm. And I've never seen the ocean."

"You're serious?"

"As a heart attack."

"Well, we'll have to remedy that."

She liked Bundy. She didn't trust him entirely just yet, but she was seventy-five percent of the way there.

They moved into another bay which was filled with supplies such as concrete and tar. Bundy examined the various boxes and bags. "Can I ask you something?"

"Depends on what you're asking. But go ahead."

"You don't seem fond of Mead, but you tolerate me. Why is that?"

It was a good question. "You want an honest answer?"

"Of course."

"Because I know I can outrun you."

Bundy stared for a moment, then burst out laughing. His deep, jovial chortles made Mina smile and laugh a little, too. It had been a good, long while since she laughed. That bumped him up to eighty percent trustworthy. Maybe even eighty-five.

"Well, ho-leeee shit," Bundy muttered.

He stared at something behind her, and her first instinct was to think it was a zombie and panic. But as she started to run, Bundy caught her arm and held her gently.

"It's okay. Nothing for you to be scared of."

He took her by the shoulders and turned her toward what held his fascination.

"Is that..."

"It sure is. Let's keep this between us for a little while, all right?"

She thought that was a good idea. "I'm okay with that. Anyway, I'm hungry. How about you?"

Bundy gave another wide grin. "Look at me, Mina. I'm always hungry."

CHAPTER TWENTY-NINE

By the time Ross returned to the truck and found Josiah eating away at his father's arm, the boy had devoured a wad of flesh the size of a racquetball.

Ross only stared at first, and when he got words out, they came out in screechy whistles through his gapped teeth, "Whaaaat the heeeeeell?"

Grady's eyes fluttered and opened. The pain was exquisite, and he walked a tightrope between consciousness and darkness.

He felt Josiah's teeth pull loose of his arm. Then he saw the boy stand and move away from him.

In his delirium, it looked like Josiah was skipping. Just an average, healthy American boy enjoying the sunny weather on a spring day. Maybe he was off to play a game of hopscotch or red rover with the friends he never had.

Then Grady saw Ross running. And then he saw Josiah catch him. The boy grabbed onto the older man's spare tire. His tiny fingers sunk into the fat and held tight.

Grady's head drifted backward and came to rest on the concrete, where he stared up at the perfect blue sky.

What a beautiful world God has given them, he thought as Ross squealed like a pig being slaughtered outside of Grady's new field of vision. We won't foul it up this time, Lord. We'll make everything right again.

Another, weaker squeal came from Ross. It sounded wet, like he might be choking. Grady barely noticed. He saw a wispy "t" of clouds high above him and thought it looked like a cross. Another sign.

After a few minutes, Ross stopped squealing, and some time after that, Josiah returned to his side. Blood had painted his face red, and only his perfect, white teeth stood out amongst the crimson mask. Even his eyes were bloody.

The boy stared down at his father, his mouth twisted into a grotesque grimace, which Grady took for a smile.

"All is well, my son. God is protecting us."

Grady sat up, and Josiah took a seat in his lap. Grady held his son in his arms and paid no attention to the mangled corpse eight yards away.

He glanced at his arm. Blood oozed from the wound, and he noticed a small puddle had formed beside him.

Grady assumed he would soon transform into a zombie, like his beautiful boy. He welcomed this first death because this death was necessary. It was only after the first death that he could be saved and welcomed into God's new kingdom.

Josiah had already been saved. The peace he displayed as Grady held him was proof of that. Before this, the boy would have never allowed even the briefest of embraces, let alone being cradled in his father's arms. God had cured the boy from the demons of autism that had tormented his short life, and he was now one of God's chosen ones.

Away from them, Ross rose to his feet and stumbled about, trying to get his legs under him. He turned toward Grady and Josiah, then did a one-eighty and shambled away in the other direction.

Grady laid in the street, holding his son, and waited for death. But death wasn't coming for him.

"THEY'RE ZOMBIES!" Dash said as he peered through the 4x-scope- attached to the hunting rifle he'd found in an abandoned pickup earlier that morning.

Bolivar had stopped the car a hundred yards from the tractor-trailer that blocked the road. He saw the two figures in the street and planned to find a way around them, but Dash was a full steam ahead kind of guy and insisted they clear the path. Aben considered himself simply along for the ride and didn't offer an opinion either way.

"Let me look." Bolivar took the rifle from Dash and held the scope to his eye.

In the distance, he could see a man on the road with a boy cradled in his arms. Neither moved. "I think they're dead."

Dash reclaimed the gun. "They aren't. Hell, you can see the kid's eyes are open. There's blood all over his face. Little fucker's a zombie!"

"No shooting until we're certain," Bolivar said in a tone of voice that made it clear this wasn't up for debate.

Dash removed his finger from the trigger and screwed his face up like a toddler who'd just been told he wasn't getting dessert. "Well then, how abouts you walk up there and ask 'em what the hell's going on?"

"I have an idea," Aben said from behind them.

The men looked at him, shocked. Aben hadn't been much of a talker thus far. Aben leaned into the car, where the dog was sprawled across the backseat.

"You know how to speak, buddy? Can you bark for me?" The dog climbed into a sitting position and wagged its tail. "Give us a bark. Speak!"

The dog threw back its head and gave two shrill yips. Aben scratched its head. "Good boy."

Bolivar and Dash watched the man and child. At first, nothing happened. Then, slowly, the boy stood up.

His body moved stiffly, like an old man waking up from a long nap. He caught sight of the men watching from afar and staggered toward them.

The man sat up next. He looked around aimlessly, his head rocking to and fro.

"Told you. Zombies!" Dash said.

Bolivar couldn't take his eyes off the boy. He was so small, almost frail. But he knew from the boy's horrible robotic walk that he was dead. He nodded. "Go ahead."

Dash licked his lips and lined up the cross hairs over the boy's face.

GRADY COULDN'T UNDERSTAND why he was still alive. He was certain that he was going to die. Maybe he was dead and just hadn't realized it yet.

He looked around, his tired eyes struggling to adjust to the bright light of day. He thought he'd heard something. A dog?

He still felt like himself. Is that how this worked? He was so confused.

Grady noticed Josiah wandering away from him and tried to reach for him, but the boy was beyond his grasp. He tried to speak, to call his son back to him, but his lips were dry, his tongue stuck to the roof of his mouth.

He attempted to summon up spit so that he'd be able to make words. Come to Daddy, he wanted to say. Come back to me.

And then Josiah's head exploded.

It seemed to happen in slow motion. A spray of black liquid. White shards of skull soaring like pieces of a shattered dinner plate. Clumps of dull, gray brain raining down.

The little boy's body stood there for a moment, his tiny fists opened and closed. Opened and closed. Grasping at nothingness. And then he collapsed.

Grady suddenly had spit in his mouth, and all he could do was scream. "Nooooo!"

"OH, Christ on a pony, what the fuck is going on?" Dash said as he watched the man he'd thought was a zombie run to the dead boy. The man scooped up pieces of his brain and shoved them into what remained of his head.

"My God..." was all Bolivar could get out.

The man gathered together bits of bone and hair and tried to sculpt it into some semblance of a head, but everything from the boy's nose up was gone.

"Oh, fuck." Dash ran his hands through his buzz cut and rocked back and forth on his feet. "Oh, fuck, oh, fuck. Make him stop that, Bol. He's gotta stop doing that."

The man unleashed a scream so mournful that it sent goosebumps racing across Bolivar's flesh. "No!"

"Should I shoot him?" Dash asked.

Bolivar turned to him, angry at first, but when he saw Dash's face had lost all its color and that his eyes were brimming with tears, the anger vanished. "No. Just sit down and wait."

Dash did so without another word. Bolivar and Aben exchanged a pained look.

"You saw him, right?" Bolivar asked.

Aben nodded. "The kid was dead. Had to be."

They looked back at the carnage and saw the man clutching the headless boy in his arms, his entire body convulsing in sobs.

"Will you come with me? I don't think I can do this alone."

Aben nodded again. "Of course."

The two of them went to Grady, who had yet to see them. Bolivar knelt at his side. "Sir. Sir, can you look at me?"

Grady stared at his twice-dead son until Bolivar put his hand on his shoulder. When he met his gaze, Bolivar immediately regretted that. The man's eyes were bulging and full of pain. His face was contorted into a mask of agony.

"Josiah." He didn't say anything else, but his arms squeezed the boy's body even harder than before, and Bolivar realized that was the boy's name.

"Was he your son?"

Grady gave one small nod and fell silent, aside from the weeping.

Bolivar couldn't stand looking at him or the dead boy any longer. He turned to Aben. "What are we going to do with him?"

Aben, too, looked away from the broken man. "What a cocked up mess."

Bolivar didn't say anything. That summed it up perfectly.

After several minutes, Grady had either exhausted himself from crying or gone catatonic. The men couldn't determine which.

Aben pried him away from Josiah's corpse and led him to the car. Along the way, he noticed the bite on Grady's arm and pointed it out to Bolivar.

"You think his kid did that?"

Bolivar saw that the wound was large but dotted around the edges with small teeth marks. He nodded. "I'd say so."

"Then why hasn't he turned?"

It was a good question, but Bolivar couldn't answer it. Everyone he'd seen bitten thus far had become a zombie in short order. He wished he could talk to the man, but his eyes were as vacant as a zombie's. Maybe it was a delayed reaction.

"It would probably be wise to bind his hands and feet. Just in case."

Aben nodded in agreement. After doing that, they deposited Grady into the back-seat of the car. Dash turned his head so that he didn't need to look at the man whose son he'd just murdered.

They headed south.

CHAPTER THIRTY

Ungrateful assholes, Mead thought as he sped along the road. He was tempted to keep driving and never return. Just let that bastard and his new girlfriend fend for themselves. Bundy was probably down to a handful of bullets. When he ran out, where would they be without Mead to save the day? Fucked, that's where.

As tempted as he was to drive solo into the sunset, the warehouse was a good location. One he had found. Why should they get to reap the benefits of his hard work? After he'd spent an hour checking every square inch of the warehouse, he returned to the lobby to see Bundy and Mina practically making out on the couch.

In the morning, they were both still asleep when Mead woke, ready to hit the road and scavenge. He was fine with his hockey stick, but they needed weapons. He also knew they needed more food since the night prior, Bundy and Mina had treated their meager supplies like a smorgasbord. Mead had felt like he was back at the restaurant.

That morning, he'd given Bundy a hard poke in the chest, and the big man's eyes fluttered. Mead asked him if he wanted to come along, but Bund only grunted and said, "Maybe later." Mead didn't bother addressing the woman who had gawked at him like he was suffering from a full-body herpes outbreak the whole night prior.

Mead was fine being on his own. At least, that's what he told himself. As the speedometer crept over a hundred miles-per-hour, he saw the zombies.

There were dozens of them, all crowded around a dinky, six-room roadside motel with a blindingly bright yellow roof. He didn't know why they were all so eager to chill at the yellow roof inn, but that didn't matter. He needed to take out his frustration on something.

The Pirelli tires shrieked as Mead skidded to the stop at the outer edges of the pothole-ridden parking lot. He was out of the vehicle and armed with his stick before the engine could stop purring.

The zombies hadn't missed his grand entrance, and the mass of them shuffled in his direction. Bring it, fuckers.

The leader of the pack was a bald man in mechanic's overalls. Mead trotted toward him, twirling the stick end for end like a cheerleader in a halftime show, and as soon as it was close enough, he sliced the zombie's head off.

Next up was a woman with a yellow name tag reading, "Beth - Asst. Manager," and with the knife end of the stick, he punched a ticket through her forehead. After that, he did a sweet spinning move and killed two zombies, one on each end of his weapon.

After Mead mowed through twenty of the creatures, he saw two men vacate a motel room. They ran toward an old Bronco, and the younger of the two dove into the cab.

They're going to run off after I did all the hard work? Is everyone who survived this plague an asshole? He was starting to believe so.

Another zombie moved close enough to kill. This one was a teenage boy with a messy coif of hair and ridiculously good looks. The kind of guy who had made Mead's life miserable in school. Probably rich, too. The prick.

Mead slammed the shaft of the stick into the zombie's face and took great pleasure in feeling the reverberations of the breaking bones. It felt so damned good.

He stood over the teenage zombie, raised the stick above his head like a spear, and slammed the knife end through the kid's nose. Not such a pretty boy anymore.

Mead glanced up and saw seven more zombies moving toward him, but just as he moved in to keep fighting, a gunshot rang out, and one fell. Then another. And another. And another. In less than ten seconds, they were all dead.

Mead saw the younger of the two men leaning against the Bronco. He set aside his rifle and gave Mead a big smile and wave as he jogged toward him.

The other man, who Mead thought looked almost old enough to get a "Happy Birthday" on the *Today Show*, followed, albeit much more slowly.

The white man looked like a country bumpkin with his flannel shirt and generic blue jeans, but when he reached Mead, he gave him an embrace strong enough to make his ribs hurt.

"We thought it was time to say our goodbyes!" the man he would come to know as Wim said. "You saved our lives. No fooling."

When he released Mead, the other man had joined them. He didn't hug Mead, and for that, Mead was grateful. They did shake hands, though. "I'm Emory, and this is Wim. Thank you."

"Mead. And you're welcome." Their gratitude was obvious. It felt good. And well deserved. "How'd you get trapped in there?"

Wim shook his head, a sheepish look clouding his otherwise happy face. "My stupidity. We holed up for the night, and I let all the guns in the truck. We didn't see any zombies when we got here. I don't know where they all came from."

Mead thought back to the fiasco at the town where he had almost cashed in his own chips. "They have a way of doing that."

Wim looked at Mead's weapon with admiration. "That's pretty incredible. I never would have thought of that."

I should be with men like this, Mead thought. Smart people. Not thankless shitheads. "I've got a lot of mileage out of it."

"I bet," Wim said. "You were downright amazing."

Amazing was an adjective that wasn't typically associated with Mead unless it was followed up with something like "failure" or "fuck up" or "loser." He grinned like the Cheshire Cat.

That smile faltered when the old man spoke up.

"Are you alone, or have you met others?"

Lie. Tell them you haven't seen anyone else. Say you've been on your own. The others don't want you anyway. You know it's true.

But as angry as he felt over their treatment of him, he couldn't bring himself to abandon them. "I met a guy a few days ago. Bundy. And then we came across a woman in an ambulance. They're a little helpless, though."

Wim's eyes grew wide as saucers. "The woman, is she about eighteen?"

That's a weird question, Mead thought but didn't say. "No. She's older. Around forty, I'd guess."

"Oh."

Mead thought the man looked disappointed, but he recovered quickly.

"Well, it's great there are more people out there. Me and Emory were starting to wonder."

"Yeah, they're the only two people I've found alive since this shit started." Aside from Wang Jie, of course, but he preferred not to think about him. "They're holed up in a warehouse maybe twenty miles from here. I've been out scouting the area, gathering food and supplies."

"You're a good man," Emory said.

Don't I know it. "Thanks, but I'm just doing what needs done. Do you guys have a plan? A place to go? Anything like that?"

Wim gazed down the road, and Mead could tell he had a mission of some sort. "We're heading further south. Down through central West Virginia. After that, we'll see."

Mead thought he was holding back, but that was okay. It was smart. They'd just met and didn't know if they could fully trust each other yet. But Mead's gut told him to give them a chance. Shit, they were better than the two buffoons he was stuck with; that was for damn sure.

"Why don't you follow me back to the warehouse? It's a good place to get prepared and rest up."

Wim and Emory exchanged a look and nod.

"We'll take you up on that, Mead. Thank you," Wim said.

"Anytime. People need to watch out for each other."

The men climbed into the Bronco and fired it up while Mead returned to the BMW. He did a U-turn and led the way.

CHAPTER THIRTY-ONE

"Stop the car, Bol. I'm so damn hungry I could eat a horse and chase the jockey," Dash said from the passenger seat.

The sign ahead read, "Save-A-Bunch Grocery," and it appeared abandoned.

"Can't you wait a while? At least, until we need gas?" The tank was three-quarters full, and Bolivar thought they had a good chance of reaching the Greenbrier without needing a refill. The longer they drove, the more anxious he became to discover what or who they might uncover there.

"I'll be quick. But I gotta get something in my gut."

Bolivar was still angry at him for shooting the boy. He knew the anger was irrational. The boy was already dead. But the aftermath made it all so terrible. He blamed it on Dash for being trigger-happy. That was easier than blaming himself.

Aben leaned forward, poking his head between the seats.

"Go ahead and stop, Bol. All I've been able to feed this mutt for the last couple days is junk. It could use some actual dog food."

When Bolivar stopped the car, Dash bounded out and found the door unlocked.

"It's open, boys!"

"Obviously," Bol said.

Dash disappeared inside, and Bol looked to Aben in the backseat.

"You go on. I'll wait here and keep watch."

While they disappeared into the store, Bol checked on Grady. The little man sat as still as a scarecrow. They'd removed the ties binding him a few hours ago, content in the belief that his window for turning into a zombie had closed.

The man allowed his limbs to be manipulated like a doll and didn't respond in any way. He only stared ahead, vacant. The man had carried no wallet or identification, so Bol had no way of knowing his name was Grady O'Baker. All he knew was that the man's catatonic state was both tragic and unnerving.

Bol had little in the way of mental health training. All of his education was of the "patch up their body so they can get back to fighting" variety. He wondered if it was possible for a person to become so distraught in grief and shock they simply went blank or whether that was a fabrication of the movies. He leaned toward the latter, but this man was changing his opinion.

While the others shopped, Jorge flopped into the backseat. The dog laid between them, its head on Grady's lap. Bol reached down and petted it. It looked up at him with big, worried eyes.

"Looks like you've got a buddy here."

Grady remained silent and motionless.

"Are you thirsty?"

No response.

Bol held the bottle to Grady's lips and tilted it slightly. Water leaked into his open mouth. He instinctively swallowed, but more fluid dribbled out of his mouth than went down his throat. Bol gently wiped away what spilled.

"Sorry about that."

He noticed there were still smears of blood on Grady, so he took a cloth from his pocket, whetted it, and cleaned him up. As he did, he rambled.

"I can't imagine the pain you're feeling. That was the most horrible thing a parent could see happen. I don't know if there's a way to recover from that, but if there is, we'll be here for you. We won't let anything happen to you. I promise you that."

He checked the bite wound on Grady's arm. It had stopped bleeding, and a dark clot now filled the ragged crevasse. He wrapped it back up.

"I'd say you're going to be just fine," he said. "Physically, anyway." The last part rushed out in a whisper.

He stared into those blank eyes. They weren't the dead eyes of a zombie—the pupils dilated and constricted—but they were every bit as blank. Bol waved his hand in front of Grady's face. Nothing. He snapped his fingers. Nada. He sighed and patted the man on the shoulder.

"If you're still in there, then I want to ask you to hang on. Things will get better."

Bolivar left the back-seat, closing the door behind him. He looked into the market and saw Dash and Aben through the big floor-to-ceiling glass windows that lined the storefront.

Dash had a shopping cart filled to the brim, and he was still browsing. Aben had a fifty-pound bag of dog food slung over his shoulder, and in his remaining hand, he carried an extra large dog bowl with rainbow-colored paw prints all over it.

Bol popped the trunk of the car and took the bag from Aben when he exited the store. He slit the top open with his knife, then held his hand out for the bowl with a raised eyebrow.

Aben smirked. "Don't judge me. It was this or pink."

"If you say so."

Bol poured some food into the bowl, and the noise of it drew the dog's attention. It popped its head out the window, and both men heard its tail thumping against the seats. Bol handed the half-full bowl to Aben.

"It's your dog. You do the honors."

Aben did, and the dog gobbled it up. "Guess he likes this more than snack cakes."

Aben leaned his back against the car while the dog ate. Bol joined him, and both waited for Dash.

"He say anything?" Aben asked with a slight nod toward the backseat.

Bolivar shook his head. "I think he might be gone."

Aben remained silent for a while, then spoke again. "It surprises you sometimes what people can come back from. Don't write him off just yet."

"I hope you're right."

"I don't know," Aben said as he stared toward the clouds in the sky. "Hell of a thing to live with. Don't know if I'd want to."

He had a point, but being a breathing shell was pretty awful, too.

"Your buddy there," Aben nodded toward the market, "This is gonna be real bad for him."

"I know."

Aben looked at him, and Bolivar felt he was being examined. Because he was. "No, you don't."

Aben turned his body so that he could look at Bolivar without having to strain his neck. "I know that makes me sound like an asshole, and I might be. Hell, almost certainly am. But you don't know. And I don't want you to take it like I'm judging you because I'd give my right hand to have been a medic like you and keep my gun in its holster all the time. Unless you're some fuckwit like Charlie Manson or John Wayne Gacy, killing is almost as hard on you as it is on the person you killed."

Bolivar thought of poor tormented Gwen Peduto, who went to her grave distraught over a good deed gone horribly wrong.

"I'm just saying, Dash is a kooky son of a bitch, and I know he can get on your last nerve because he gets on mine, too, but we need to cut him some slack."

"Okay. I will."

"Good." Aben suddenly grinned, and the expression completely transformed his face. "You didn't even crack a smile when I said I'd give my right hand. That's a pretty big deal, considering it's the only one I got." He tapped Bolivar's shoulder with his stump.

Just as Bolivar smiled back, Dash vacated the store, pushing his overloaded shopping cart like it was a racecar. He almost crashed into them before pulling it back under control.

"I stocked us up good, boys!" He started tossing food into the open trunk. Canned goods mostly, but also cereals, various drinks, and a box of something in small jars.

"What's that?" Bol asked.

"Oh." Dash popped open the box and pulled out a jar. "Baby food."

Bolivar looked at him like he was crazy, and even Aben had trouble masking his confusion.

"It's for him." Dash pointed to Grady inside the car. "I know it sounds goofy, but I don't want him to go hungry, so I thought this might work. Least until he gets better."

Dash's eyes were brighter than they'd been since the shooting, and he made Bolivar think of a little boy waiting expectantly for his teacher's approval.

"Did I do good, boys?"

Bolivar felt a pang of regret for being so short with him, for blaming him. None of this was Dash's fault.

"Yeah, Dash. You did real good."

Dash's crazy grin made a triumphant return. "Hot damn!"

He tossed the remaining groceries into the trunk. They almost filled it to the brim. "Let's blow this joint, brother!"

They did just that.

CHAPTER THIRTY-TWO

Mead didn't believe in love at first sight. He didn't believe in love at all, truth be told. It was for fools. Nevertheless, as he watched the girl beat in a zombie's head with a cinder block, he felt his heart swell up just like the Grinch.

His luck with cars was the worst, and when the BMW he'd been driving shit the bed a few hours earlier, he wasn't even surprised. The rest of the group had gone a different direction earlier that morning. So far, their scavenger hunts hadn't borne much fruit. Canned goods and a few old guns were the extent of it.

Mead headed into a valley that he'd previously passed by. He had a good feeling about it. But soon, something in the wheel's well started thudding so hard he could feel the vibrations in the steering column. Eventually, the thud turned into a metallic screech as the wheel locked up.

He found he didn't really care about being stranded there all alone. He had his blade, and he needed that more than other people. Maybe he'd catch up with them again, and maybe not. No great loss.

He had wandered a few miles when he saw the old Indian cruiser motorcycle leaning against a rundown mobile home. The bike's worth more than the entire house, he thought. As someone who grew up as trailer trash himself, he was confident in his judgment and wondered how they'd afforded such a nice ride. Probably had a seized engine. Not that Mead knew what that even meant.

There was no key in the motorcycle's ignition, and he thought about continuing down the road for an easier ride to grab, but he liked the look of the bike, and it was all too easy to picture himself riding down the highway, the wind whipping through his long hair. Maybe he'd become skilled enough that he could swing and decapitate zombies without even slowing down. The fact that he'd never ridden more than a dirt bike—and that was over ten years ago—didn't deter him in the slightest.

The rickety steps groaned underneath him as he climbed to the trailer door. Before opening it, he grabbed his stick and held it ready at his side. When he pulled the thin, metal screen door open, the hinges squealed and shattered his attempt at stealth.

The mobile home was old and rundown but relatively neat. The only items out of place were a smattering of baby toys scattered across the floor. It felt empty, but Mead stayed alert as he sifted through the kitchen drawers, hoping to find the keys to the Indian.

After digging through silverware, screwdrivers, and miscellaneous junk, he came up empty-handed. On to Plan B.

When he stepped into what passed for the master bedroom, his attention drifted to a poorly posed family photo hanging askew on the wall. In it, a man and woman, both in their early twenties (younger than me, he thought), sat in front of a fake flower backdrop. In the woman's arms was a baby.

They might have made it, he thought, even though he knew it wasn't true. Mead hadn't seen his own kid in years and rarely gave the boy any thought, but looking at that crappy picture made him wonder what might have happened. He pushed the thought aside, not because it was too hard, but because it was pointless, and continued his search.

He hit pay dirt in the underwear drawer where a skull key chain holding two keys rested underneath some worn-out boxers. After dropping the keys into his pocket, he moved into the hall, where he paused outside a closed door.

When he pushed the door open, he found what he expected; a nursery. The daffodil yellow walls were cut in half by a clown border, which was glued to form a makeshift chair rail.

Tucked into the back corner, just below the window, was a wooden crib. Mead considered turning back several times, but his curiosity got the best of him. It was a bad idea.

When Mead reached the crib and looked down at the white satin-lined bedding, he saw a scrawny, gray, and very zombified baby staring up with dead eyes. When the baby saw Mead, it let loose something between a growl and a goo goo. Thick, yellow drool drained from its toothless mouth, and it waved its tiny limbs at him in awkward, circular swipes.

He stared at it for a long moment before trying to raise the hockey stick. The blade hit the low ceiling, and he realized he didn't have enough room to maneuver it. Instead, he set the stick aside and pulled a Bowie knife from his belt.

The undead baby kept swinging its hands at Mead's descending arms, and the blade of the knife nicked its tiny pinky finger. Black blood oozed from the wound like tar. Mead pushed its little arm aside, and the baby hissed as it raised its head off the bedding and tried to bite him.

Mead pushed its head back against a blanket, which was covered with ducks and chicks, and held it firm. Its jaws kept biting as Mead touched the tip of the knife against the center of the baby's forehead.

He pressed down and was surprised when its thin, still malleable skull popped like an egg shell, and the blade sunk into the baby's head up to the hilt.

The baby stopped moving, and Mead pulled the knife free. He used the bedding to wipe the black gore clean from the blade, then returned it to his belt.

Movement outside the narrow bedroom window caught his

attention just before he could leave the room. A woman lumbered across the lawn in that awkward, staggering gate of the undead. He grabbed the hockey stick.

As Mead hit the front door, the zombie reached the steps. She looked up at him, and he recognized her from the family photo on the trailer wall. Vacant, hopeless death had replaced the glow of motherhood, and her oversized maternity shirt still pouched outward with baby weight she'd never lose.

He swung the stick, and it arced through the air in line to take off her head, but before the blade could connect, the woman stumbled forward and smashed face first into the metal steps.

Mead had been expecting his blade to meet resistance, and when it caught nothing but air, it became embedded in the metal siding of the trailer. He tried to jerk it free, but the damned thing was stuck.

As he worked to extract the stick, the zombie grabbed hold of his ass and caught her hand in his back pocket. Her weight pulled him down, and he did a back flip over her before crashing onto the hard ground.

While Mead rolled onto his belly and scrambled to his knees, the zombie came for him. He brandished the same knife he'd just used to exterminate her baby and lunged at her.

The blade of the knife entered her face just to the right of her nose, and the handle stuck out like a pin in a voodoo doll. It hadn't penetrated deep enough to destroy her brain, and she flailed with her arms, smacking him in the face and digging at his head.

"Damn it, bitch!" he said with a grunt as he tried to catch the knife's handle. "Hold still!"

She thrashed beneath him, and he was running out of energy to hold her at bay. Multiple days with nothing to eat but gas station junk food and energy drinks had kept him awake but left him ill-prepared for prolonged physical altercations.

He lucked out when the dead woman also ran out of steam. Her thrashing head slowed enough for him to catch the handle of the knife, and, with his remaining strength, he pulled it loose.

Mead took his time and slid the blade into her eye. He kept pushing even after the eyeball popped and sent a warm spray of fluid the color and consistency of curdled milk back into his face.

He pushed until the handle disappeared into the socket and only stopped when the blade met resistance at the back of her skull. Mead wasn't sure when she'd stopped moving, but the woman was dead. Again.

He laid on top of her and tried to catch his breath, but just seconds later, a long shadow fell over him, and he heard a raspy groan.

"Motherfucker."

He rolled off the dead woman, catching his cheek on the ragged edge of a metal step and slicing his face open in the process. When he looked up, he saw the hayseed father from the family picture coming at him.

Dad hadn't fared as well as his family, and he had two big bites taken out of his neck. Hickeys from hell. His wounds didn't slow him down, though, and in seconds, he was at Mead's feet.

Mead pushed himself backward until he hit the skirting of the trailer. His stick was buried in the wall. His knife in the woman's face. He was helpless.

He pushed against the skirting, hoping to get it loose enough to crawl under the mobile home, but it was tight and held firm.

With the zombie in striking distance, he kicked out with his right foot and connected with its knee, which buckled backward with a crunch. It teetered for a moment, then lost its balance and started falling right at Mead.

Mead didn't have time to think of his never-ending shitty luck before the zombie landed on top of him. Pinned between the metal skirting and the zombie, Mead was spent. There was no strength remaining with which to free himself from this latest jam.

The zombie snarled, and when it opened its mouth, Mead could smell rot and death spilling from deep inside it. The smell sent his stomach into spasms, and he felt puke rushing up his throat. He didn't bother turning away, and the hot vomit burst from his mouth and sprayed the zombie in the face projectile-style.

The monster growled and hissed as Mead's stomach acid and chunks of half-dissolved Twinkies and Ho-Hos slid down its face. The sight was enough to make Mead smile. He never imagined death would look so horrible and amusing at once.

The creature leaned in toward him, their faces just inches apart, but Mead was finished. He had no energy to fight. He waited to get eaten.

That changed when the zombie's lower jaw disappeared in an explosion of black blood and shattered teeth.

Mead and the zombie looked sideways in unison like synchronized swimmers. They saw a girl, who looked no more than twenty, holding a pistol. She shot again, and the bullet hit the zombie in the ribs and sent it careening sideways, off of Mead.

"Damn it!" She sprinted toward Mead and the monster. When she reached them, she aimed the gun at the back of the zombie's head and pulled the trigger. And nothing happened. She tried again. Nothing.

Mead was so shocked by these developments he didn't even have time to think a derisive thought about why guns made such poor weapons.

Instead, he watched as the girl grabbed a broken cinder block from beside the trailer, raised it above her head, and brought it down on the zombie's skull. It crumpled inward with a crunch that sounded like a hundred eggs being cracked at once.

She wasn't done, though. She raised the concrete block again and swung it for round two. Most of the zombie's head was in pieces on the ground, and when Mead looked from the destroyed zombie to the girl's beautiful, pixie face, he realized he was in love.

CHAPTER THIRTY-THREE

SOLOMON FLIPPED UP THE SMOKED GLASS SHIELD OF THE welder's mask. He'd worked up quite a sweat underneath it, and the drops had painted pinstripes on his blood-covered face so that it alternated back and forth. Blood, flesh. Blood, flesh.

His headache had mostly gone away. He'd always found work to be a calming force. Focusing on a singular task made his other problems go away. Apparently, that worked even when you had two holes in your noggin.

Saw looked at his creation, as proud as a new papa. The Kenworth dump truck, the pride of his operation, had been transformed into a killing machine. He'd welded twelve-foot lengths of rebar to the front, where they jutted out to form long spears. On the sides, he'd welded row upon row of razor wire left over from an old construction job in a high-crime area.

He filled the sleeper cab with sledgehammers, demo bars, and various shears and cutting tools. He even added a few chainsaws for good measure. It was ten tons of rolling death, and he couldn't wait to put it to use.

He watched his reflection in a shop mirror as he unwrapped the bandage from his head. The holes in his skull had stopped leaking blood, but he knew they still had the potential to become infected.

He lit a road flare and watched his face turn candy apple red in the glow. Saw held the flare against the bullet wound in his forehead and counted to five. When he pulled it away, he revealed a charred hole. He thought he looked like he had a third eye. A pitch-black cyclops.

"Let's see now. I spy with my little eye... destruction." He grinned, revealing nearly all of his rotten teeth.

Solomon Baldwin felt like he'd been waiting his whole life for a scenario such as this. A time when he could let his true self show.

Fuck all of society's niceties and rules. Man was meant to fight. Laws, morals, only stopped the strong from reaching their true potential and protected the weak. The sheep. Now, there was no one to hide behind. Now, the world would belong to those who were willing to fight for it. Now, he could fully become Saw.

SAW WANTED to test his dump truck turned weapon. He headed toward a shopping mall parking lot, where zombies staggered across the acres of asphalt.

He cackled as he drove toward them, hitting the first few at twenty miles an hour. The zombies that didn't end up skewered on rebar spears fell under the dump truck's heavy wheels, where their bodies broke and burst. The creatures which collided with the sides of the truck became swept up into the coils of razor wire and were dragged along.

He kept it up for fifteen minutes, never losing his horrible smile. He noticed that the zombies at the front of the truck were piled in deep, packed onto the rebar like beef and peppers on shish kabobs. He grabbed a sledgehammer from the passenger seat and hopped out of the cab.

Eight zombies were caught up in the wire on the driver's side.

When they saw Solomon, they growled and stretched in an attempt to grab him. The razor wire cut deep into their flesh, and black blood oozed out.

"Hold tight, mates. I've got plans for you, but I want to take care of the chaps up front first."

He strolled to the cab, where around thirty zombies had been impaled through their chests and torsos. They hung off the metal rods like ventriloquist dummies, their arms and legs flailing.

"Looks like you folks got yourselves in a sticky wicket."

He moved within a yard of them. The creatures desperately tried to snatch him, grabbing at the air, clawing at the other zombies trapped with them. To Saw, their guttural gasps and hisses sounded better than the Mormon Tabernacle Choir.

Solomon lifted the hammer end of the sledge from his shoulder, looked at the nearest zombie, and swung. Its head imploded, splashing out clods of brains. Some ricocheted into Saw's face. That made the whole ordeal even more exciting.

One by one, he beat in the heads of the creatures stuck to his dump truck, and when he was done, they hung there like slabs of meat. He took his time removing them, and when finished, he'd produced a sizable pile of destroyed zombies. It had all worked just as planned. The apocalypse was proving to be buckets of fun.

CHAPTER THIRTY-FOUR

THE TOWN HAD NO STOPLIGHTS, JUST TWO STREETS THAT intersected in a roundabout with a picturesque white gazebo in the center. It seemed empty, save for two zombies that wandered about and a third sprawled across the steps of the library. He looked like a wino missing his paper bag cloaked bottle. As the rumble of an engine approached, the zombies turned in the direction of the sound and waited.

Against his best instincts, Bol allowed Dash to drive when he became road weary, and Aben refused. As they rolled into town, Dash slammed on the brakes, almost launching Bolivar into the windshield. In the back, the dog tumbled off the seat but bounced up again, wagging its tail like it was enjoying the experience. Aben gave it a rough scratch on the head.

"What the hell, Dash?"

Dash pointed to a nearby storefront. Bolivar followed his gesture and saw a sign reading, "Barrow Bros. Sporting Goods."

"Figured we should stock up," Dash said and jogged toward the door.

Bolivar looked to Aben. "It's probably not a bad idea."

Aben nodded and motioned to the three zombies, which moved toward them from across the circle. "You go ahead. I'll take care of them."

Bolivar moved toward Dash, who had reached the door, while Aben exited the vehicle. Aben glanced at Grady through the half-open window. The little man stared straight ahead but saw nothing.

"You hold tight now."

Grady didn't respond, not that Aben expected him to. He hadn't said a word since they picked him up, and, deep down inside, Aben believed all three of them preferred it that way.

Aben looked at the dog. "You, too." The dog wagged its tail even faster. At least, it listened to him.

At the shop, Dash tried the door and found it locked.

"Aw, hell," Dash said and gave the door a hard shove, rattling it in the frame.

Bolivar reached above the door jamb, feeling for a key, and came up empty-handed. He bent to check under the mat, but Dash pushed him back. "I got this."

Dash raised his booted foot and planted it firmly under the doorknob. The wood door screeched and cracked but didn't give way. A second kick did the job. He looked to Bolivar with that goofy grin. "Who needs a ke—"

His words were cut off when an alarm sounded. It was a sharp, high-pitched shriek that pierced the air so violently that the men had to cover their ears.

"What the hell?" Dash said. "There's no power!"

"Must be on a battery backup."

They could barely hear each other through the screaming alarm, but what was done was done, and they entered the store.

ABEN HAD REACHED the first zombie, a middle-aged woman in cut-off denim short shorts and an American flag tank top. Her blonde hair spilled down over her shoulders and hung halfway down her back.

She was the type of woman he would have looked at twice, maybe even three times when she was alive. But now, there was a gaping hole in her bare midriff, and that pretty much ruined the effect.

He glanced toward the sporting goods store, where the alarm was making his head hurt. When he turned back to the sexy, undead patriot, she was only a few feet away.

He let her come to him before bringing the hammer down on her skull. She grunted and stumbled sideways, tripping over an upraised section of the sidewalk, and then fell to the road.

A young man in a pizza delivery boy uniform wasn't far behind. He made Aben remember, not fondly, of pizza face—the girl who had gotten him thrown in jail and nearly killed. He strode toward the teen and slammed the hammer into the zombie's forehead. He felt the concussion through the handle as the skull broke. Pizza boy went down in a heap.

Aben looked to the third zombie, which stumbled toward him from across the street. It was an eighty-something-year-old man, bent at the waist by age, but dried blood around his mouth showed he was far from harmless. Aben clutched the hammer in his hand and walked toward him. Time to put the old timer out of his misery.

What Aben didn't see were the arched double doors of the church beside which they had parked, swing open and the zombies come pouring out.

CHAPTER THIRTY-FIVE

Ramey didn't know what to think of the greasy man she'd saved outside the mobile home. He said all the right things and appeared genuinely grateful, but something in his face made her wonder. It was the way he looked at her. Not like she was a fellow human being, but more like how a dog looks at a discarded bone that it wants all for itself.

Stop it, she told herself. You're being weird. He's probably just scared like everyone else. And maybe that's all it was, but she was glad she had Peggy and wasn't alone with him, just in case.

It had taken Mead several attempts to start the old motorcycle, and once the engine was running, he almost toppled over twice as he tried to roll forward. He kept glancing back at her and Peggy, an awkward and probably fake smile plastered to his face.

"Just a little rusty." He got going eventually, and they followed behind in the pickup.

"He's a squirrelly one," Peggy said, and Ramey thought that was an accurate summary.

"Yeah. But he's alive."

"I suppose that counts for something."

Mead told them he'd been traveling with others but had broken off on his own to go scouting when his car died. Something about the way he told the story made both women uneasy. His eyes would meet Ramey's own, then dart away as if he was stealing glances at an eclipse.

She thought maybe it was her own fault—that she might be staring at the swollen, pus-tinged zits that dotted his forehead or the gash on his face—and knew it wasn't fair to judge him based on a few minutes of interaction. Maybe once they caught up to the other people he'd been with, he'd be more relaxed.

As they neared a stretch of road, off of which a sprawling farmhouse and barn stood, Mead hit the brakes on the motorcycle and did a little shimmy in the middle of the road. The bike hopped sideways before slowing to a ragged stop. Ramey saw a vehicle on the road and, past it, twenty-plus zombies.

Ramey watched through the windshield as Mead eased the bike onto its kickstand and stepped off. He pulled his strange hockey stick weapon off his shoulder and walked.

"If nothing else, he's brave," Ramey said.

Peggy watched, her fingers digging into the armrests. "Stupid people usually are."

IT HAD BEEN Wim's idea to check the farmhouse. It reminded him of his own abode, although this house was much larger, easily two, maybe three times as big as his now abandoned home sweet home.

Bundy and Mina went to check the barn and outbuildings for supplies. Wim turned to Emory, who was busy eating a black banana he'd pilfered from a house earlier that morning. He extended it to Wim, who shook his head.

"Might be your last chance at fresh produce."

Wim looked at the banana. "Fresh?"

"Perhaps fresh was an improper adjective, but still... beggars and choosers and all that."

"I'm fine. Thank you." Wim shut off the truck and grabbed his rifle. "You wait here until I make sure the coast is clear."

"I'll do no such thing, William. I'm old but not entirely feeble." Emory grabbed one of the revolvers and was out of the Bronco before Wim could object.

They climbed onto the porch, and Wim pushed the front door open. It swung inward, unimpeded. That opened into the kitchen, and Wim hoped they'd find some jarred meat.

He'd already grown tired of canned tuna and chicken, and just the thought of beef or venison got his mouth watering fiercely. But they needed to make sure the house was empty before the snooping could commence.

All the rooms on the ground floor were empty. The upstairs was a repeat. Emory discovered an old Flintlock muzzle loader mounted on the wall and pointed it out to Wim.

"Should we take this?"

"Oh, geez, I haven't shot one of those in twenty years. That's one step up from what they used in the Revolutionary War. If we're that desperate, I'd say we might as well curl up and die."

Emory grinned. "I defer to your knowledge."

They returned to the first floor and rummaged for food. They found some but nothing great. And certainly no meat. Wim noticed a door in the corner. He'd been in enough farmhouses to know it led to the root cellar.

Wim reckoned there was a good chance for fruit and vegetables down there. And maybe... no, he was finished getting his hopes up.

As he turned the porcelain doorknob, a gunshot came from outside.

Emory looked out the kitchen window. "This looks like a pickle."

Wim joined him at the window, and when he looked toward the barn, he saw a dozen or so zombies shuffling out of the barn doors and into daylight. Before he could react, the cellar door opened.

When Wim and Emory turned, they saw a group of Amish zombies filing into the kitchen.

"This is like the ice cream all over again," Wim said.

"Pardon?"

"Never mind."

Wim shouldered the rifle and started shooting. He took out three of the zombies, but the rest closed in too quickly. The creatures were going to overrun them fast if they lingered.

"Get out!" he shouted to Emory, who obeyed, scurrying out of the door.

Wim backed out of the kitchen. He shot one more and dropped it. He saw at least six more coming and slammed the door closed, but it only bounced in the frame. As the two men fled across the lawn, the zombies followed.

BUNDY HAD FALLEN in a mud pit and was sunk to his knees. Two zombies that had wandered out of the barn approached. Their feet also plunged into the muck, but they managed to trudge ahead.

Mina remembered the little pistol she had tucked in her pocket. Bundy had been giving her shooting lessons and said she was a quick learner. But there was a difference between shooting oil cans and moving targets. And it was especially different when you could stand there and be calm about it versus when it mattered in a life and death situation.

She fired her pistol and hit a zombie but only connected with its chest. The monster didn't flinch. A second shot went wide, and splinters of wood exploded from the barn wall.

Shit, she thought, this is so hard. "Why even bother? You can't do nothin' right, Birdie," her daddy's voice echoed through her head. Maybe he was right, but she didn't want to hear it.

She steadied her shaking hands, aimed again, and fired. The third shot pierced the zombie's head, and, as her daddy often said, it dropped like a whore's drawers. "What do you think of me now, Daddy?" she muttered.

Bundy dug through the mud, trying to find the gun he had dropped when he fell but had no luck. The second zombie was two big steps away from him. Mina shot again and missed again.

"He's gonna die, Birdie. This is all your fault," her daddy cackled. "You got him killed. Hope you're happy with yo'self."

Mina aimed the pistol, steadying herself. She aimed it at the zombie's head, held her breath, and pulled the trigger.

The gun only clicked.

In her head, her daddy laughed and laughed.

CHAPTER THIRTY-SIX

As Aben swung the hammer at the old man, a gunshot rang out and startled him so badly that he flinched in mid-swing. The hammer only caught the zombie's nose. It folded over sideways like a piece of putty.

He turned toward the sound of the shot but forgot about looking for the source when he saw dozens of zombies shuffling out of the church, down the steps and into the road by their vehicles.

The old zombie took advantage of Aben's attention being diverted and grabbed a handful of his long, stringy hair. It pulled his head back, toward its gaping mouth. Aben could hear its jaws snapping together and thought it an odd, plastic sound. Dentures, he assumed.

Aben spun around and lost a clump of hair in the process. It ripped free from his skull, and he saw a chunk of bloody skin hanging from the root end, but he paid it little attention.

He smashed the hammer into the zombie's mouth, and his suspicions were confirmed when big chunks of fake teeth and pink dental plate fell free from its broken jaw.

He reared back with the maul, this time slamming the pointed end into the zombie's temple. Its head burst open and black brains fell out as it hit the ground.

Aben turned back toward the horde of zombies, toward his companions. He saw Dash fire three more rounds. Bolivar raised his pistol, fired two quick shots, and Aben saw a zombie's head explode. He ran toward his new friends.

BOLIVAR AND DASH found plenty of guns in the sporting goods store, but all were locked in display cases with glass that looked thick enough to support the weight of an elephant.

"We need that damned maul of Aben's," Dash said and moved toward the exit.

Bolivar doubted that the hammer would break the glass. He suspected it was bulletproofed. Looking for a key was a better plan. He did just that until he heard Dash mutter something unintelligible through the shrieking of the alarm. That was followed by a gunshot.

Bolivar ran to the exit and saw Dash standing just outside the doorway, rifle pressed against his shoulder and aiming it in the direction of over forty zombies. They filed out of a gray, stone church, which, if the ornate stained-glass windows were any indication, was Catholic.

They must have gone to church when they got sick, Bolivar thought. Went there to pray for forgiveness and salvation but died inside instead. It gave him a pang in his heart as he thought about all the Sunday mornings he'd spent at Mass, somewhat bored but also in awe of the spectacle of it. He'd even considered becoming a Priest one time but never felt the calling was strong enough to commit.

When Dash killed three more zombies, Bolivar snapped out of his introspection and used his pistol to kill two others. They'd made a small clearing, and Dash took the opportunity to make his move.

"We'll flank 'em!" he said as he ran toward the gazebo. He bounded up the steps in two large gallops and steadied the rifle against the railing. Dash picked off zombies one by one, never missing a headshot, and Bolivar had to admire his aim, if not his sense.

Bolivar saw Aben loping toward him, the hammer clutched in his hand in a death grip.

"My pistols are in the car!" Aben said as he joined Bolivar outside of the shop. The path to the car was blocked by zombies. "Did you get anything inside?"

Bolivar shook his head. "Everything's locked tight. Try to break the locks."

Aben ran into the shop, and Bolivar covered the door. He shot a girl that couldn't have even made it to her teens and watched her pigtails whip black blood through the air as she spun in a circle and fell to the ground. He heard a crash inside the shop and looked back to see Aben standing at a gun case where the lock was damaged but still holding.

"Not gonna keep me out, you bastard," Aben said and raised the maul high over his head. He brought it down with all the strength he possessed.

As Bolivar watched his wild hair fly from the effort, he thought Aben looked every bit the part of a deranged Viking. Or a Norse God. The hammer connected with the lock, which fell to the floor in pieces.

Bolivar rushed back into the shop and loaded a pistol for Aben. His hands quivered as he shoved ammunition into magazines. He realized he was absolutely terrified.

CHAPTER THIRTY-SEVEN

MEAD WASN'T SCARED AS HE APPROACHED THE ZOMBIES. THIS was his chance to prove himself with Ramey watching. She'd saved him from one zombie, but now it was his turn to save her from dozens.

Doubt didn't even lurk in the deep recesses of his consciousness; he knew he could do it. He'd kill the fuckers and win her heart. It would happen. He was sure of it.

He noticed all the zombies were dressed alike. The males wore plain black trousers and white shirts. The women ankle-length dresses. Amish zombies, I'll be shit, Mead thought.

He spotted Wim's truck ahead, as well as the ambulance, but saw none of the people he'd left behind earlier that morning.

He wondered if they were all dead. He'd miss Wim and Emory, but at the same time, being the sole hero—the savior—had a certain appeal. That daydream dissipated when he heard a gunshot crack. Zombies don't shoot guns, so at least one of them was still alive.

Four children and two adults shuffled toward him. He noticed two of the kids were girls who looked like twins. They had long blonde hair pulled up in buns and covered with a bit of white cloth. When he chopped off the top of the head of the first girl, that covering went soaring through the air, along with a large chunk of skull and hair.

He swung the stick like a sword and lopped off the entire head of one of the adults, an Amish woman. Her skull rolled across the street, where it got caught up in the feet of other incoming monsters, whose shuffling legs kicked it to and fro like a soccer ball.

Mead then impaled a zombie through the eye, jerked the stick free, swung around, and spilled the intestines of another. It fell onto its knees, and he shoved the knife end of the stick straight through its nose and deep into its skull.

Three more zombies were close by, and they walked in a single file line toward him. Mead ran at them, holding his stick at waist level like a jousting lance.

It pierced the stomach of the first, then the second, and finally the third, forming a zombie kabob. He took a moment to snicker at the absurdity of it as they attempted to walk. They reminded him of foosmen, and he thought he should retrieve the severed head for them to punt.

He grabbed a knife from his belt and stabbed the first through the eye. It dropped and pulled the other two with it, making them easy pickings.

He stabbed both of the others in their temples, then pulled his stick loose. It was covered in putrid, black zombie innards, and his gloved hands became coated and slippery with them.

When he swung at the next zombie in line, the stick slid free from his grip and went skittering across the road. The zombie was within arm's reach, and Mead grabbed for a knife, but before he could get it, a gunshot rang out so loudly that he thought he might go deaf. The zombie's face collapsed inward at the bridge of its nose, and it fell.

Mead looked and saw Ramey a few feet behind him, her pistol raised. Peggy was a yard or so back, holding a shotgun they'd found earlier in the day. Mead had no time to thank the girl because more zombies were on the move.

MINA JUMPED into the mud pit, or maybe it was manure. It certainly stank. Her small, light body didn't sink as deep as Bundy's or the zombie's. She worked her way to the creature and grabbed its coarse gray beard.

"Get away from it, Mina!" Bundy shouted.

But she wouldn't do that. If she chickened out, her daddy would win, and she was tired of that bastard winning. Mina pulled the zombie forward, and because it was in the mud up to its calves, she had the advantage.

The zombie fell face first into the mud, and Mina dove onto its back. She forced its face into the foul, brown filth and didn't stop until its entire head was buried. Then she took the pistol, raised it high over her head, and swung it down.

The grip connected with the zombie's skull. She hit it again. And again. And again. After another blow, she realized the pistol had broken a hole in the back of the monster's skull.

She sat back, catching her breath. Bundy crawled toward her, each move a heavy, sucking thwack as his limbs broke free of the mud. He sat beside her, atop the zombie. She realized he was staring at her.

"What?"

"You've got a little something." He tapped his face.

Mina felt hers and realized she was covered with mud, blood, and brains. She tried to wipe it away, but the same mess was all over her hands, and she only made it worse.

Bundy laughed. "Never mind." He leaned over, took her chin in his huge hand, and pulled her face close to his. "I think it's pretty damned sexy myself."

He kissed her, and she let him. Take that, Daddy.

WIM WATCHED as Mead slaughtered three more zombies. The man was merciless. When he finished, he was covered in black, rotting gore. Mead turned to make sure the area was clear and saw Wim looking down on him.

"Good work, buddy."

Mead nodded. "Thanks."

Wim handed Meade a handkerchief, which the younger man used to wipe the blood from his weapons. "Good to see you again. We have to stop splitting up."

Mead nodded. "Yeah. That would be wise."

They surveyed the grounds of the farmhouse, which appeared free of zombies. Wim saw Bundy and Mina approaching from near the barn. Emory waited by the Bronco, and Wim thought his hands were shaking.

Wim noticed that Mead appeared almost frantic as he looked for someone or something.

"What's the matter?" Wim asked.

"I found two women," Mead said, ignoring the fact that they had actually found, and saved, him. "A girl and a woman. But I don't see them now. Where the hell did they go?"

The explosion of a gunshot answered the question. Wim and Mead ran toward the sound of gunfire.

When they reached it, they saw Peggy standing and two bodies on the ground. Mead let out a low, pained groan.

Peggy turned when she heard him. She had the shotgun at her hip and her finger on the trigger.

"Whoa!" Wim called out. "It's okay."

Peggy lowered the gun. "Scared the shit out of me!"

Mead ran toward her. No, he ran past her. To the two bodies on the ground. A zombie, missing its head from the jaw up, was on top of a woman. Wim watched as Mead grabbed the dead creature's shirt and ripped the corpse away from her.

The woman coughed, her breath hitching. She was covered in gore, and Wim couldn't make out any of her features.

"Jesus! Jesus, I thought you were dead." Mead wiped some of the remnants of the zombie's head off her, his hands clumsily rubbing across her chest. She swatted him away.

"I'm fine. Thanks to Peggy."

That voice. Wim was certain he knew whose voice that was. He told himself it was his imagination playing tricks again. Not to get his hopes up.

Mead grabbed her hands and pulled her to her feet. She grabbed her midsection, cringing.

"I think that bastard broke a couple ribs when he landed on me."

Wim swallowed hard. He couldn't believe it. He half wondered if he was asleep and this was a dream. Then Ramey saw him.

"Well, looky there, it's Wim Wagner. Of all the people to find in West Virginia."

There was still a heavy spatter of blood on her forehead and her top lip was split, but she looked good. Better than good. She ran to Wim and threw her arms around him, hitting him so hard that he stumbled backward a step.

"I feel like my damn chest is gonna split in two, but I don't even care," she said.

Wim remembered her comment about the ribs and quickly let go, but she held on to him. "I owe you a box of bullets."

"Aw, don't worry about that."

She squeezed his hands as she looked into his eyes. "I never thought I'd see you again, Wim. I'm so glad I was wrong."

Wim couldn't hold back a grin and felt his cheeks heat up as a blush spread across them. "I'm glad you were wrong, too."

They'd both forgotten Mead existed, and neither of them noticed him watching with a look on his face like his world had just imploded.

CHAPTER THIRTY-EIGHT

JULI STOOD IN FRONT OF A FLOOR-TO-CEILING MIRROR AND looked at her reflection. The outfit she modeled, khaki trousers and an emerald-colored button-down blouse, looked good on her. She no longer cared that her figure had changed dramatically over the last decade. She was blissful to finally be free of the blood-soaked nightgown.

She'd come upon the little town by accident. A big truck had rolled on its side on the freeway, so she had taken a detour of random back roads. As her Audi rolled into town, she was surprised to see the streets lined with upscale boutiques. Everything from clothing to jewelry stores to craft shops.

It was the kind of town she used to visit with Mark on the weekends when he was off work and the kids were off doing whatever they did with their friends. And now, she didn't even need her gold card.

Juli window shopped until she saw the lovely clothing store. The entry door featured teal paint that had a perfect patina. She walked back to the Audi, took the tire iron, and returned to the shop. She felt rather guilty as she pried the door open, but it was easier than expected.

You did it now, Juli Villarreal. Breaking and entering to add to your laundry list of recent crimes. You're quite the master criminal.

She smiled a little, and smiling felt nice. She felt even better when she stepped inside and saw rack after rack of women's clothing.

Over the next hour, she shoplifted a new wardrobe. She had six outfits picked out when the alarm went off. It startled her so bad that she felt a hot squirt of pee come out before she could stop it. Now I'll have to find another pair of pants, she thought.

But she was scared. Had she set off the alarm? Why was it only coming on now? She wanted to hide and wait for it to stop, but a part of her expected the police to arrive and arrest her.

They'd tell her everything she thought she'd experienced the last few days was a mental breakdown or a fugue state, that zombies weren't real, and she was an insane woman on a murder spree. The jig was up. To the slammer, she would go.

Juli grabbed the tire iron and held it tight as she stepped to the door. She didn't realize she was holding her breath until it all came out in a gush when she saw the postcard-pretty town square, which had been empty an hour ago, was full of zombies.

She stood in the open doorway, white-knuckling the tire iron and praying she didn't have to use it. Then she saw the car. She was sure it hadn't been there when she arrived. And zombies don't drive, so that must mean there was a person—or maybe persons, plural—in town, too. Gosh, how she wanted to see another living person. The thought of it forced her from the shop and onto the sidewalk.

Juli saw the dog first. It reminded her of a terrier/lab mix she'd had growing up. Cinnamon. That dog was her best friend, and she desperately missed having a four-legged companion.

Mark was allergic, an ailment he had passed on to their kids. He wouldn't even allow a hypoallergenic dog. Pets were out of the question, and she had obeyed. Maybe she could have a dog now that her family was dead. As far as silver linings went, that was rather poor, but she clung to it nonetheless.

Juli watched as the dog snarled and snapped at zombies that reached into the partially open windows. It chomped on the hand of a dead man in a baseball cap who pulled back three fingers instead of five. Good for you, pup. I always enjoyed finger sandwiches, too.

As she moved closer to the car and the dog, she saw a man in the backseat. From behind, he appeared motionless, maybe even dead. He reacted not at all as the zombies clawed and grabbed at him.

Juli saw one of the zombies grab the dog's ear, and the dog let loose a short, pained yip as the monster pulled on it. The man didn't try to help, but she did. Juli ran to the vehicle, swung the tire iron back like a tennis racket, and treated the zombie's head like she was serving. The sound as the metal connected with the zombie's skull both sickened and excited her.

It fell against the car, then slithered down the side until it hit the ground and remained motionless. She rammed the pry end of the iron through the eye socket of another zombie, and it, too, dropped.

The next one in line was a teenage boy, and as soon as she saw him, she thought he looked like a less handsome version of her Matt. That made her wonder if Matt had ever escaped the house and, if he had, whether someone had killed him.

She couldn't fight this Matt-lite zombie. She couldn't bring herself to do it. Instead, she opened the car door and dove inside. The dog jumped into her lap and licked her face, and Juli didn't even care that its muzzle was covered in black zombie blood.

The man didn't react. She thought he might be dead, but his chest rose and fell in steady, peaceful breaths.

"Is someone else here with you?"

Nothing. It was a stupid question anyway. Of course, someone else was with him. He didn't drive here while sitting in the backseat. He still hadn't acknowledged her presence in any way.

"Hey, are you okay?" She sat her hand atop his. It was like touching a mannequin.

Her mind reeled with questions about this shell of a human being, but she became preoccupied with the zombies that surrounded the car, pressing against it, clawing at the windows. As far as hiding places go, this one sucks, she thought.

DASH RAN out of ammo with nine zombies still surrounding the gazebo. There was a gap wide enough that he thought he could fit through it if he timed it right.

"Now or never," he muttered, mostly to himself.

He hopped over the wooden railing. The eight-foot drop knocked some of the wind out of him, and he landed with an "Oof" and stumbled to one knee.

He got back up and ran, passing by a zombie he'd shot earlier. As he stepped over it, the zombie reached up and caught hold of his pant leg. Dash stumbled and fell on top of it. His now useless rifle went flying.

A small hole dotted the zombie's left cheek. A much larger hole opened up on the right side of its face where the cheekbone and eye socket used to be. The wound was grotesque, but the brain was unharmed.

The zombie clawed at Dash. One hand caught his shirt collar. The other, his ear. It dragged him downward, toward its destroyed face. Its jaws snapped and bit air.

Bolivar realized the shots from the gazebo had ceased. When he looked, he saw Dash was missing from his sniper's perch. He found him a few yards away, just in time to see the zombie underneath pulling their faces together.

"No. Damn it, no," Bol said. He raised his pistol and tried to aim, but they were so close, their heads only inches apart, that he didn't trust himself to take a shot.

Dash used his left arm to try to hold the zombie at bay, and with his right, he fished for a knife in his belt. His hand brushed the hilt. His fingers fumbled with the snap as he tried to free it. Still, the zombie dragged him nearer. He could smell the rancid breath spilling from its mouth.

Dash unsnapped the strap, and his hand closed over the handle. He pulled it loose, but before he could use it, the zombie got his face close enough to bite. It locked lips with Dash in an undead French kiss, its jaws chomping, biting. Blood gushed from between their two mouths.

Dash tried to scream through their locked lips. He brought the knife up and plunged it into the zombie's ear. The blade sunk in until the guard collided with the creature's skull.

Another zombie grabbed onto Dash's head and pulled. That broke the bottom zombie's bite, and, when their faces came apart, Dash was missing both his lips. When he opened his mouth to scream again, a ragged bit of tongue extruded and gushed dark, almost purple, blood.

Bolivar shot at the zombie who was holding on to Dash's head. Missed. He fired again, and the bullet caught the creature in the sternum.

It was too late anyway as the other zombies fell onto Dash like linebackers piling on a QB. Soon enough, he stopped struggling. Bol couldn't watch anymore and turned away.

"Damn it."

Aben stepped out of the store and followed his gaze. Dash wasn't visible under the mass.

"Dash?"

Bolivar nodded.

They surveyed the scene. Aside from the creatures eating Dash, there were now twenty or so zombies left standing, and most of them flocked near the car. It was only then that Bolivar remembered Grady. "We need to finish this and get to the car."

"And my dog," Aben added.

Bolivar holstered his pistol and took a rifle that Aben had

extended to him. One by one, he killed the zombies that were eating Dash.

Aben had a pistol of his own. They marched toward the remaining zombies, shooting as they walked.

They shot again and again until only four zombies were left standing, all near the back end of the car. The creatures scratched and clawed, fighting to pry their way inside.

Aben heard the dog bark. "Get away from him, you assholes."

He ran straight into the group of them. He pressed the barrel against the head of a middle-aged man in a WVU t-shirt. When he squeezed the trigger, the man's skull exploded across the side window. Aben spun, shot another zombie in the face. It dropped. Next, he shot and killed a woman in a floral print blouse.

The last of them, a teenage boy in a McDonald's uniform, had his arm extended into the car. It tried to pull away, but something inside was holding it. Is it the dog? It sure as hell can't be Grady, can it? Bol thought.

"Kill it!" a woman's voice inside the car shouted.

Bolivar and Aben exchanged confused glances, then Aben shot the teen in the back of the head. Bol peered inside and spotted the new arrival. She waved.

Before the men could react to her presence, Aben noticed Dash approaching from the diamond.

"Aw, Christ," Aben said.

Bolivar followed his gaze and saw Dash. Most of his lower face had been eaten away. Bites had been taken from his neck, arms, and torso. His clothing was torn and bloody. And his eyes, of course, were dead.

Aben moved toward him, pistol in hand, but Bol grabbed his shoulder.

"No. I'll do it." His voice wavered.

Aben looked at Bol. "You don't have to."

"I do."

Bolivar took a few steps toward the approaching zombie. This was worse than Peduto. She was dead. Or still dead, anyway. Not up and moving. But the raspy growls coming from what was left of Dash's mouth were proof enough that whatever had made him human was gone for good.

He thought about saying he was sorry, but that would have only been for his benefit. It wouldn't make a difference to Dash.

Bolivar aimed and fired, and Dash was dead.

CHAPTER THIRTY-NINE

After surviving the debacle at the farm, Wim and the others returned to the warehouse. Everyone had gone their separate ways except for Wim, Ramey, and Emory, who sat alone in an office and talked about everything except zombies.

Wim was happier than he'd been since his animals died. This felt right. These people felt right. He was optimistic that maybe the worst was over and they could start their lives anew.

Emory had been regaling them with more stories of his travels. "And that's how I ended up stark naked in the Seine!"

They all laughed, especially Ramey. She'd been giggling a lot this evening, and Wim loved the sound. A wide yawn cut short Emory's own chuckle.

"My, the hours are catching up to me. I should retire for the evening. I trust you two young people will get along fine without a chaperon?" He raised an eyebrow and looked from Wim to Ramey.

"I'm sure we'll be just fine." She crossed her heart.

Emory stood and gave a dramatic little bow. "Then I bid you both adieu." He reached out, took Ramey's hand, and gave it a light kiss. "I'm so very happy I had the opportunity to meet the young lady

Wim has been going on about. Now that I have, I can understand why."

Ramey laughed again, and Emory left the room. When it was just the two of them, Wim suddenly found himself struggling for words. He tried to think of something to say but came up empty-handed. When he looked at Ramey, she was grinning.

"Do I make you nervous?"

"What? No. Of course not. I don't know why you'd think that."

She watched him, still grinning, and silent.

He attempted to lick his lips and found his mouth dry as powder. "Yeah. A little."

She cast off another lilting titter, and he couldn't hold back a smile of his own.

"You shouldn't be nervous. I'm just a girl. I'm not scary."

Ramey slid across the tile floor until she was sitting next to him. She leaned back, resting against his broad chest, grabbed his hand, and pulled his arm around her shoulders.

Wim felt as if his entire body was on fire, and his stomach twisted into hard knots, but he surprised himself by enjoying it. He liked the way Ramey's chocolate-colored hair felt against his neck and how her soft hand fit into his calloused palm like a piece of a puzzle. The only thing that worried him was whether she could feel his heart pounding. If she did, she didn't say anything.

"I'm sorry I ran off like I did. I never thought you'd leave the farm. And I was afraid, if I stayed too long in that quiet safety, I wouldn't be able to leave, either."

"I understand. I know you need to find out what happened to your dad. And I'll get you there and keep you safe. I promise."

"I believe you. I don't think you could tell a lie if your life depended on it."

"I..." He lost his words again.

"You don't have to say anything, Wim." She gave his hand a squeeze. "Just don't let go of me, okay?"

They fell asleep like that.

Mead liked to wander, always had. He could never sit still in class. Couldn't stay at a particular job or apartment for too long. He needed to be moving all the time, like a shark. He spent most of the night haunting the hallways and using a flashlight to explore the various rooms of the warehouse.

He eventually worked his way toward an employee break area, where he planned to use some road flares he'd found to heat up a can of ravioli.

He couldn't believe his shitty luck. What were the odds that the girl he fell for was the same chick Wim had been hunting all over Timbuktu and back? Shit like that only happened to him.

He kept telling himself that maybe they were just good friends. Hell, maybe Ramey viewed Wim as a father figure. The dude was no spring chicken. Sure, Mead was only a couple years younger, but at least he hadn't hit the big 3-0 just yet. Don't freak yourself out. Just keep showing Ramey how awesome you are, and she'll come around.

As he headed toward the break room, he saw them. Wim with his stupid flannel-shirted arm wrapped around Ramey's shoulders. Her head laying against his chest as they slept. She still had her hand in his.

He lost his appetite. The tower of lies he'd been telling himself crumbled. What does that hayseed bastard have that I don't? He was plain and boring. Probably spent his life screwing sheep or maybe, if he was lucky, his inbred cousins. And she falls for him? It didn't make sense. Life didn't make sense.

Since Mead was a boy, he'd always felt like the stranger in the crowd. The person looking in from the outside. It started in kindergarten when, on the first day of class, he walked up to another boy and asked, "Wanna be my friend?" The boy said, "No."

It stayed that way his entire life. He was the kid the bullies singled out. He was the kid who never got chosen for class projects until the teacher made the others take him in. He was the kid who ate his lunch alone every day while the others pointed and laughed. It didn't make sense because he was never cruel. He was a nice person.

Mead was tired of being nice. He was finished giving people the benefit of the doubt. They always let him down. And he was sick of being treated like shit all the time.

This was a new world, and he wasn't going to be a doormat anymore. And he sure as hell wasn't going to save the lives of people who didn't appreciate him.

Fuck 'em all.

CHAPTER FORTY

MITCH HAD SPENT DAYS TRYING TO IGNORE THE BODIES HE'D tucked away in a corner of the control room. He couldn't ignore the smell, though. It reminded him of the summer he'd bussed tables at a high-end restaurant. His father's idea. "Get the boy a job and teach him responsibility."

Part of his duties involved taking out the trash and depositing it in the dumpster. The smell that had invaded the control room wasn't far off from how the dumpster smelled on the hottest August days. He tried to pretend that it wasn't his mother who was now smelling the same as rancid pork and rotten vegetables in the summer heat.

He was an orphan. He'd felt that way much of his life, but now it was real, and he still wasn't sure how to react. So, he watched the monitors where zombies shuffled from room to room, bounced off walls, and tripped over discarded furniture.

He wondered if they were hungry, too. They hadn't eaten in days, either. Everyone that had been alive was long gone. Except him. And he wasn't going anywhere.

Mitch glanced away from the monitors and watched a few zombies that ambled outside the control room. Occasionally, they'd see him, approach the glass, and bounce off like bumper cars. One of them was Mitch's father. He'd been sticking around the room for the last day, and Mitch wondered if any sense of recognition remained.

Mitch pressed his face against the glass as his dead father approached and eventually smacked into it face first, his nose bending obscenely to the side. He looked into Mitch's eyes, bared his teeth, and growled.

"Right back at ya, Pops."

While the two stared each other down, Mitch thought about how much he'd hated the man. He never inspired respect or fear, let alone admiration. He was a career-obsessed asshole who used Mitch as a prop to further his own ambitions. All he had felt for him in life was hatred. Looking at him now, in death, he found the old man to be downright pitiful.

"Where did all of your focus groups and polls get you, Pops? Rotting away in a bunker with all your asshole cronies. You're dead, and I'm just fine. Bet you never saw that coming."

Mitch tapped the glass, and his dead father went crazy. He banged and clawed at the window. More zombies, roused by the commotion, joined in and, soon, a few dozen crowded against the glass.

Mitch smacked it again, harder. Then again. The zombies became riled up like monkeys in a zoo, and he enjoyed tormenting them.

He was having so much fun that he didn't notice the exterior cameras capture a car pulling into the Greenbrier's front lot.

THE PALATIAL RESORT was unlike anything Bolivar had ever seen. They passed through a gated entry point where, before the plague, a guard would have determined who was granted admission and who was not. After passing the guard shack, they drove up a long tree and flower-lined lane. Then the hotel came into view.

It looked bigger than the White House. Pristine, white buildings stretched out far behind it and from each side. It was large enough to house Bolivar's entire hometown times twenty. All of this tucked away amid a forest in the middle of nowhere.

A few zombies roamed the grounds, mostly soldiers or men and women in dark suits. They totaled less than a dozen altogether, and Bolivar thought it was a sign that Dash's story of a secret bunker buried beneath the resort might be true after all. Surely, if it was an ordinary hotel, there should be hundreds of zombies roaming the grounds. Rich tourists struck down while on holiday. For there to be so few meant the public portion had been evacuated.

Bolivar parked the car in a circular drive, which surrounded a garden overflowing with red tulips. He and Aben exited the vehicle. While Juli tried to coax Grady out into the open, the dog hopped out and ran around with near boundless energy.

Bol and Aben destroyed the zombies. As they returned to the car, they saw Grady out in the open air. He stood there, statuesque, but when Juli took his hand and led him toward the hotel, he trudged along. The two men exchanged a shocked glance.

"Miracle?" Aben asked.

"I'd save that word for when he speaks."

"Then I won't hold my breath."

They gathered together as many firearms as they could carry and followed Juli and Grady toward the grand entrance.

Inside, the hotel was a ghost town. Everything was immaculate and undisturbed. The black and white tile floors were spotless. Bolivar half expected an attendant to come forward and greet them.

"Welcome to the Greenbriar," Aben said from behind him.

Bolivar looked back. "It's... interesting."

The decoration was nauseatingly lavish. Every window had colorful fabric swags. Floral print covered all the furniture. The ceilings were fifteen feet high and were supported by ornately carved pillars. Every time he looked up, Bolivar saw a different chandelier.

"Do rich people really like this shit?" Aben asked.

"I think it's beautiful," Juli said.

Bol and Aben traded a smirk. They set the first round of their supplies on the floor and wandered around the lobby. Juli started up a red, black, and green carpeted staircase. Bol worked on getting Grady into a sitting position on a settee that looked straight out of Victorian England.

"Aw, shit."

They turned toward Aben's voice. He stood by the dining room and ran his hand through his stringy hair as he looked at something on the wall.

Bolivar left Grady and moved toward him. "What is it?"

"There's a dress code for dinner. Jacket and tie required. I guess I'm shit out of luck."

Bolivar laughed, a deep belly laugh that made him feel better than he had since this whole disaster had begun.

"Maybe there's one in the lost and found."

Aben laughed, too. "That's a good idea, Bol. I'll check on that."

Bolivar felt almost normal again, and even if it was only for a moment, it felt good.

CHAPTER FORTY-ONE

In the morning, hours before anyone realized Mead was gone, Bundy woke, looked to his side, and saw Mina's face only a few inches from his own. They had spent the night together in more ways than one.

It was awkward and embarrassing and amazing all at once. Bundy had been with women before, was even engaged for a few months, but the connection he felt with Mina was different and better.

Afterward, she opened up to him about her father for the first time. When she finished, he wished he could kill the man again for her. She fell asleep crying.

His heart ached for the pain she'd endured, and he wondered if she'd ever be able to get over it. Was it even possible to move on from a lifetime of that kind of torment?

The feel of all her hard angles against his flabby chest was a pleasant surprise. Her skin was like warm velvet, and he wished he never had to separate from it. He kissed her on the ear, and she smiled, half-awake but keeping her eyes closed.

"Good morning," he whispered.

She stretched out, and as he felt her warm, firm butt press against his groin, he felt himself getting hard. She must have felt it, too, because she smiled and opened her eyes.

"Too early for that, my handsome man."

Bundy had been called a lot of things in life, but handsome wasn't one of them. The pure sincerity in her voice meant even more to him than the compliment.

"Can't blame me, though. It's your fault for being so damned beautiful."

She rolled onto her back, her small breasts disappearing against her ribs.

"Thank you," she said.

"For what?"

"For being so... gentle."

Bundy traced his fingers over her waist. "I want you to promise me something."

"What's that, hon?"

"That you won't ever thank me again for treating you right. That doesn't deserve a thanks. That's the way it's supposed to be."

She put her hand on his face and kissed him.

Bundy thought again that this moment should never end.

But everything good comes to an end sooner or later. Usually sooner.

EMORY STOOD outside the warehouse and stretched away the stiffness, at least as much as possible at his advanced age. The morning was cool, and he saw his breaths create pale clouds every time he exhaled.

Some of the others had been talking about moving on and looking for larger groups of survivors, but Emory had his doubts. The plague had happened too quickly for any large group of people to have been evacuated or saved. Of that, he was certain. But he didn't mind because as he looked out at the beauty surrounding him, he felt filled to the brim with the spirit of God.

He never considered himself to be an overly religious man, but staring out at the surrounding glory made it impossible to believe it was all some sort of happy accident. No cosmic egg could crack open and spill a yolk like this. Apologies to Monsieur Lemaître, but Emory wasn't buying it.

As he stood in the silence, he saw a small whitetail deer wander out of the woods at the rear of the warehouse. It nibbled on some clover growing amongst the grass, then caught a whiff of Emory. It craned its head in his direction, found him, and stared.

"You have nothing to fear from me. Although, I speak not for my compatriots."

It took a few more bites, then bounded into the woods.

The sight filled his heart almost to the brim. This was still a beautiful world, and Emory was excited to see what the future held.

After waking up with Ramey still asleep against his chest, Wim was reluctant to move, but a rumbling in his belly got the best of him. He eased Ramey off and let her sleep as he headed into the break room, where he remembered seeing some plastic bowls.

He took some cans of peaches, pineapples, and cherries, and mixed them together, hoping it would be enough to feed everyone. As he looked out of the room's lone window, he, too, saw the deer wander out of the tree line, the sun illuminating the small rack of antlers atop its golden-brown head. They looked to still be covered in velvet, and that made him smile. He hoped there was a doe in the area, too. Perhaps life could go on after all.

He'd initially seen the plague as a curse, but maybe it was

something else entirely. Maybe it was a cleansing of the slate. A modern-day version of the Great Flood. He still wondered why he'd been spared, but now, he was happy to be one of the lucky ones. He intended to put his lottery ticket to good use. He wanted to make a difference this time around. He wanted to live, not simply exist.

CHAPTER FORTY-TWO

After he tired of harassing the zombies, Mitch returned to his swivel chair behind the TV monitors and spun around and around and around until his head was swimming. The boredom was the worst. Well, maybe the hunger was worse, but boredom was almost more than he could bear.

The zombies had dispersed again, wandering about aimlessly and doing whatever it was that zombies did when there was no one around to eat.

Mitch watched them on the monitors as they shambled around, occasionally bumping into one another and growling or hissing, then going on their separate ways again. He was bored with this show, too.

He flipped through the various cameras and almost went right past the one displaying the exterior of the resort, but the car caught his eye just before he switched it off.

"That wasn't there before."

He glanced over at the rotting heap in the corner where his mother's body was slowly dissolving. Puddles of yellow and green goo had leaked out and inched their way toward him.

He sometimes woke up at night afraid that the putrefying liquid had washed the whole way across the floor, and he'd find himself sleeping in it. Forget Liquid Plumber, this was Liquid Mother.

Mitch flipped through more camera angles and, in doing so, saw three men, one woman, and a dog inside the hotel. All appeared armed, except for the small nerdy-looking guy who sat motionless, staring at the wall.

"Jesus Christ, even the zombies have more personality than you, buddy."

While these new people looked prepared to fight zombies, they also appeared to be searching for something. They checked hallways, looked behind tapestries on the wall, and did everything except pull on random books in the library and say, 'Open sesame.'

"You're looking for the bunker, aren't you?" Mitch grinned, his eyes avid. This was good. "You're searching for the heroes, but all that's left to find is me..." He licked his lips at the thought.

He turned again toward the body in the corner.

"We've got company, Mother."

Mother didn't respond.

Over six hours of searching had proven fruitless. They'd found nothing. No zombies. No bunker. No false walls or secret passages.

Aben wasn't too surprised. If there was a top-secret bunker, it would almost certainly be inaccessible from the general hotel. But he doubted there was ever a bunker in the first place. And with even more certainty, he doubted anyone would still be alive, even if the stories were true.

He didn't share his thoughts with Bolivar because he could tell the soldier was distraught over the perceived failure. Bol had pinned all his hopes for the future of humanity on this place, and now he realized that donkey tale was wildly misplaced. Aben wasn't going to say that out loud, but he did suggest they consider moving on sooner rather than later.

"I know. We'll go in the morning." Defeat clouded Bolivar's voice.

Aben nodded. "No sense lingering."

"I don't understand the hurry," Juli said.

They both turned to look at Juli when she spoke.

"There's nothing for us here," Aben said.

Juli motioned to the floor-to-ceiling glass windows that looked out on the surrounding mountains.

"And what's waiting for us out there?" She'd been removing the dressing on Grady's bite wound but stopped as she spoke.

"Jorge said they destroyed Philadelphia and killed everyone in it. I saw what was happening in Baltimore. That was Government sanctioned homicide. D.C. is gone. Do you really think anything is different in Chicago or Dallas or L.A.? Really?"

Both men remained silent. Aben realized she had a point. He was quite confident that the country, and probably the whole world, had been wiped out. Maybe there were islands in the Pacific or villages in inaccessible parts of the Amazon where people had avoided being turned into zombies, but as for everywhere civilized... Nice knowing you. Here's a souvenir t-shirt.

"What then?" Bolivar asked. "We just sit here and do nothing but exist?"

"Is that so bad? At least, for a little while? For all we know, those zombies will die off on their own. Maybe they'll rot to pieces or starve to death if people like us aren't dumb enough to go out there and get eaten."

"She's got a point, Bol," Aben said.

Bolivar looked at him, his eyes wide. "But what about other people? People who might die without our help?"

"I'm not cut out for saving the world, Bol." Aben saw Bolivar's eyes flare and realized he needed to dial it back. "I'm just saying, it might not be a bad idea at all to take a day or so and think about things."

Bolivar gave a slight nod but didn't respond otherwise.

"The appliances in the kitchen are all gas. I'd be glad to make us something to eat. The pantries are very well stocked." Juli said.

"That sounds good."

"Watch after him for me, okay?" She looked at Grady, who sat as silent as a church mouse.

Aben gave his most reassuring smile. "I doubt he'll get up and run away, but we'll keep an eye out."

She left the room. Bol moved to Grady and busied himself with examining the wound. Aben felt he was purposely ignoring him, and that was all right.

Aben stared out the window and thought it looked peaceful. He remembered learning once upon a time that the Earth was self-healing. That's how it survived meteors and ice ages and all that shit. Ultimately, it was the people who were its biggest enemy.

Maybe this is what the world needed, Aben thought. A do-over. Sucks for everyone who died, but the idea that this was all for the best was something he couldn't shake.

CHAPTER FORTY-THREE

HARD RAIN AND VIOLENT THUNDERSTORMS KEPT THE GROUP trapped inside the warehouse for three days. Mead never returned, and that bothered Wim.

He'd liked Mead in the few days he'd been around him. Most of the others didn't appear to miss him, and that confused Wim even more than the man's sudden departure. He might have been an odd duck, but he was incredibly smart and innovative when it came to fighting and defending themselves against the zombies. Wim wanted to search for him, but the rain coming down was of the cats and dogs variety, so Ramey and Emory talked him out of it.

There was nothing to do but talk, and talking had never been Wim's strong suit. Even Emory was running out of stories to tell. Wim had gotten to know Peggy better, and he was glad for the opportunity.

She was a country girl and reminded him of his mama, only rougher around the edges. She, too, had grown up on a farm, and they discussed that commonality off and on, but like everything else, the interest wore off soon enough.

Wim knew many of them, especially Mina and Peggy, had grown

tired of their quarters. Wim didn't entirely blame them. The only options for sleep were upright in chairs or prone on the hard floor.

The warehouse was dark on a sunny day and an abyss on dreary ones. It felt like an oversized, sterile coffin. Ramey had spoken little about her father, but Wim caught her staring out of the windows for long stretches at a time and knew she, too, was getting antsy.

Their meager food supplies were dwindling, and when they woke to clear skies on the fourth day, heading out wasn't just an option. It was a necessity.

Wim's plan was to go out and scavenge again, search for Mead, then return to the warehouse to regroup in case the man came back.

He was outvoted. The majority, which included everyone except himself and Emory, wanted to say their final goodbyes. Wim didn't fancy himself any sort of leader, so he didn't object.

Ramey had informed everyone of her father's letter, and they unanimously agreed to head in that direction. As they loaded their supplies into the vehicles, Wim noticed that the steel radial belt was showing through on one of the pickup's tires. He checked, and there was no spare.

"It's not safe to drive like that," he told her.

"Well, it wasn't really my truck anyway. Just felt like it."

She agreed to leave it behind. It was funny, Wim thought, the way people became attached to their big cages of metal. He knew his own Bronco couldn't last forever but hoped to delay the inevitable as long as possible.

Bundy and Mina took the ambulance, and Peggy rode in the back. Wim, Ramey, and Emory piled into the Bronco, and they left the warehouse in the past.

Wim and Mina had been taking turns leading the way throughout the day. At present, Mina was in the lead, and he watched the back of the ambulance as it gained on him. It possessed more get up and go than his old Bronco, and she had a lead foot.

He was also growing weary of the drive. They'd stopped at a couple stores earlier in the day and loaded up on food. Bundy had even found a shotgun hidden under a checkout counter. They'd seen a few zombies and dispatched them, but it was a monotonous day.

A sign at the side of the road declared, "Coalwood - 2 mi." Ramey saw it and pulled out her map.

"That's on the map! We're getting close."

Wim glanced at the paper. She was right—they were close—but he guessed they still had twenty or so miles to go before they reached the X.

A tiny town stood in the distance. It had a single street lined with small company houses. One gas station stood on the outskirts.

He couldn't see any zombies, but he wasn't looking too hard because in his peripheral vision, he noticed Ramey dancing in her seat. It was excitement over the map. Over her father.

Wim had little hope they'd find anything where X marked the spot. He was unsure how she'd handle it if they arrived and found more nothingness and she realized it had been a fool's errand. He considered broaching the subject to possibly soften the coming blow. Before he could say anything, the ambulance disappeared.

CHAPTER FORTY-FOUR

It was morning, and Mitch hadn't slept a minute the night prior. He worried the people who had invaded the hotel would disappear if he dared fall asleep. That would be tragic because he meant to escape the bunker, and he needed distractions.

On the monitors, Mitch saw that the people in the resort had woken up and were eating. The woman fed the nerdy dude spoonful after spoonful of what looked like apple sauce.

"Christ, why did you idiots waste your time rescuing some gork?"

Mitch knew the odds of them finding their way to the bunker were slim to none. And even if they did find it, they weren't getting in. The steel doors were built to withstand a nuclear blast and wouldn't open from the outside without a keycard or the security code.

He'd have given anything for a gun. Or even a fucking baseball bat. But all there was, was the letter opener he'd used to kill his mother. That poor excuse for a weapon was still embedded at the base of her skull.

He needed it, though, because fleeing the safety of the control room with nothing was suicide. Mitch was a lot of things, but suicidal he was not. That meant he had to retrieve the letter opener. And that meant he had to look at his mother's body.

Her skin had taken on an almost transparent quality, like all of her internal bits were coated in plastic wrap. She looked like she'd gained thirty pounds due to the bloating. He had to turn her head sideways to access the letter opener, and when he pushed against her face, he felt the slimy skin slide and separate from the tissue underneath it.

His fingers sunk into her rotting flesh up to the first knuckle. He dry-heaved and felt like he was going to vomit, but after not eating for days, nothing came.

His hand darted out, and he pulled the letter opener free with a quick jerk, then he lobster crawled away from her as fast as he could.

That was intense, he thought and gave a little laugh.

As he approached the control room exit, he wiped his hands on his pants and stared at the two zombies outside the room. He mouthed, "Bring it, bitches!"

Then Mitch opened the door.

Juli had woken two hours earlier. Aben and Jorge were off exploring the hotel again and had invited her along, but she wasn't interested in poking around the same nooks and crannies as the day prior.

Instead, she decided to organize supplies in the kitchen, which was enormous but woefully lacking in high-quality cookware. When she had it sorted to her satisfaction, she moved to the room where the four of them had slept the night before.

She'd put Grady to bed like a toddler, and in the morning, he remained in the exact same position. She couldn't tell whether he'd slept because his eyes were open when she fell asleep and were still open when she woke up. For the previous hour, she'd been watching him.

Bolivar had told her about Grady's son and the name he'd spoken. Josiah. Juli's heart broke for him. The others could never understand that pain, but she could. She lived with it every moment of every day.

She talked to him off and on, but he never responded. Maybe he really is gone, she thought. Weren't mental hospitals full of people like this? People that stared into space without a thought in their heads? But if there was any part of him still inside, still aware, she wanted to be there for him.

She used a wet cloth to wash his face and arms, cleansing away the last remnants of his son's blood. The wound on his arm appeared to be healing when she changed his bandage and showed no signs of infection. The bleeding had stopped completely. Thank God for small favors.

Juli held the catatonic man's hand and prayed for him.

Mitch stabbed the first zombie in the eye. The second posed more of a challenge, and when he went to stab it, the letter opener hit its cheekbone, and the faux sword bent at a forty-five-degree angle, slicing a chunk of flesh that dangled off the dead man's face like a piece of bologna.

The zombie kept coming for him, and Mitch stumbled backward. In the process, he tripped over the first zombie and went sprawling on the floor.

His ankle twisted underneath him and sent a burst of pain up his leg. He screamed before he could stop himself.

The sound enraged the zombie even more. It dove on top of him. The rotting smell coming from its mouth was all too close. Mitch gripped the twisted letter opener in his fist and slammed it upward.

It pierced the fat flesh under the zombie's jaw, and he crammed it in as far as it would go. Then he twisted and jerked and pulled, doing his best to dice up whatever was inside its skull.

When Mitch realized the creature was dead, he pushed it off of himself and crawled to his knees. Beyond them, he saw shadows in the corridor. The shadows moved toward him, and Mitch didn't need a fancy private school education to know what was coming.

Bolivar and Aben worked their way down a long service hall. Ductwork and water pipes lined the passage, and the combination narrowed the width of the space to five feet.

"Do you really think it's over?" Bolivar asked. They were some of the first words he'd said all morning. "Humanity, I mean."

"I wouldn't say over. I guess I'm telling myself it's more a chance to start fresh. That's my glass-half-full take on it, anyway."

"What's your half-empty take?"

"That we're all fucked." He grinned. Even Bolivar gave something resembling a smirk.

"Let's go with the former."

"Let's."

The hallway seemed to be never-ending. Occasionally, they came upon a small door that opened to a closet or storage space, but mostly, it was long stretches of nothingness.

"Can I ask you a personal question?" Bolivar watched Aben, trying to get a read on him.

"No one's stopping you. That doesn't mean I'll answer it."

"You're homeless, right?"

"I believe we all are."

"You know what I mean."

"I do. And I am."

"How did you end up that way?"

Aben waited a while before responding, and Bol thought he might have overstepped his bounds, but he eventually got around to it.

"I was back stateside for a little over a year. I'd leased an apartment in the town where I grew up. Where most of the people I'd known before the war still lived." Aben checked a door. It opened to a closet full of cleaning supplies. "I didn't re-acclimate well."

"Did you have much family to fall back on?"

"Parents. An older brother, but he moved to Alaska while I was in Iraq. Haven't seen him since, actually. But when my lease was up, I decided to do one of those cross-country-find-yourself-spiritual-healing-bullshit trips. All new age-y, right? Anyway, after a year or eighteen months of that, it got to be a habit."

"Did you ever do it?" Bolivar had stopped walking and was watching him.

"Do what?"

"Find yourself?"

"Nah. But I didn't look all that hard."

Bolivar's eyes drifted past him, a few yards up the corridor. "I'll be damned."

CHAPTER FORTY-FIVE

BUNDY RAN HIS HAND OVER MINA'S THIGH, PUSHING IT CLOSER and closer to that magical spot between her legs.

She swatted his hand playfully. "Do men ever think about anything but sex?"

Bundy continued caressing. She wouldn't admit that it felt good, and she secretly preferred he didn't stop.

"I'm not thinking about sex. I'm thinking this is a damned boring trip. It's my duty to do something to spice it up."

"Oh, really, now?"

They zipped past the "Coalwood - 2mi" sign. Mina's heavy foot had the ambulance flying at almost seventy miles an hour.

"You like spice?"

"I love it. Hot sauce. Habaneros. Damn, I'm getting hungry again."

His hand was between her legs now. His fingers worked overtime. She gave a little shiver and squeezed her thighs together, trapping his hand there.

"Stop! I don't want her to see," Mina whispered with a head tilt to the rear of the ambulance.

Bundy looked into the back and grinned. "Peggy's sawin' logs. We may as well be alone."

That suited her just fine. She let her legs come apart so that his fingers were free. "So, what are you hungry for?"

"I'm not picky. If your food is half as hot as you are, I'm a lucky man."

"It don't matter if I can cook or not. You're already lucky."

"Believe me, I know it."

He removed his hand from her crotch, an act that disappointed her. She wanted to tell him to put it back, but before she could say that, he grabbed her chin, turned her face toward his own, and kissed her.

"What the hell?" Ramey screamed.

The ambulance seemed to have vanished, like a magician had passed a cloth in front of it, waved a magic wand, and sent it to some other dimension. It had been there one moment, gone the next.

"What happened?" Emory asked from the backseat. He'd just woken from road-induced slumber, and his voice was groggy.

Wim slowed the Bronco. He was fifty yards from where the ambulance had disappeared. Then, he saw smoke. He slowed further: twenty miles-per-hour, ten, five. What had begun with a few wisps of white steam had become billowing gray clouds.

He was only a few feet from the gaping crevasse in the road when he saw it. The pavement was completely normal, then it dropped off into nothingness.

"The road washed out," Wim said as he jumped out of the Bronco. To his left, he saw a deep gash in the mountainside where water funneled down. Three days of rain was too much for the hollow to handle, and the steady flow had created a chasm twelve feet wide and over twenty feet deep.

"Oh shit! Oh shit!" Ramey said.

He hadn't even known that she'd arrived at his side. He was too busy staring into the hole in the ground where the ambulance had landed nose first.

Along with chunks of asphalt and fallen trees, the crevasse was filled with hundreds of zombies. Wim couldn't tell if they'd been washed into the hole during the storm or if they'd fallen in afterward. It didn't matter much how they got there because they all flocked toward the ambulance.

"I have a tow rope in the back of the Bronco. Get it," he said. As Ramey sprinted back to the vehicle, he got down on his knees and peered over the edge.

"Mina! Bundy!" He waited for an answer, but none came. The ambulance looked unharmed aside from the smoke pouring out of the smashed radiator.

He prepared to drop over the edge into the hole, but before he could do that, the rear door of the ambulance flopped open.

CHAPTER FORTY-SIX

The ramp incline was long and steep, and Mitch struggled to catch his breath and keep moving. His sprained ankle was on fire, and the only thing that kept him going was the steady chorus of growls and groans that serenaded him from behind, like an undead band that wouldn't shut the hell up.

Every few steps, he looked back. He knew it was slowing him down, but he couldn't help it. Each time he glanced backward, more zombies had come close enough to be seen and the thunder of their encroaching steps filled the corridor to a deafening level. Mitch believed every zombie in the bunker was giving him chase. A thousand cats and he was the mouse.

How much further is it? His legs felt like jelly, and for the first time in his life, he wished he'd have put more effort into gym class. Finally, in the distance, he saw the door. The zombies were closer than ever. Their stench filled the corridor. The smell was so oppressive he could taste death in his mouth.

Mitch smacked into the door, too exhausted to stop the collision. He swiped his key card and waited. At first, nothing happened. He tried again. Still nothing. Of course, a general access card wouldn't open the primary entrance. He should have known that. How could he be so stupid?

The zombies were closer. He could feel the concrete floor vibrating under his feet. I never should have left the control room. I should have stayed in there and starved to death. It would be better than this. He stared back at them as they rambled along. There was no need to hurry. Mitch was trapped.

Aben followed Bolivar's gaze and saw what held his attention. The hallway ended in a large, steel door with a glowing keypad beside it. Aben jogged to it.

"We should get Juli," Bolivar said

"Why? Because she knows the secret code?" Aben grinned and randomly pressed numbers.

"Because she should know we found it. This is why we came here, right?"

"I suppose." As Aben continued mashing at the keypad, the door unleashed a groan. They looked at each other in surprise and confusion.

"That was easier than expected," Aben said.

Bolivar raised his eyebrows. "That didn't actually work, right?"

"It's opening."

And it was. The door slid sideways an inch at a time and disappeared into a slot in the wall. When it had opened less than two feet, a boy slithered through the opening and fell to the floor.

Bolivar first thought he was a zombie. His skin was stretched taut across his face and his eyes sunken into their sockets. But when the boy looked at them, Bol realized he was alive.

"Jesus, kid," Aben said. "You look like shit warmed over."

The boy stared up at them confused, but his confusion morphed into fear. "Run."

"What?"

"Run!"

The door continued to open, and Bolivar heard something behind it. Movement. It grew louder. And then he heard the growls. He peered into the tunnel. In the dim green fluorescent light, he realized that the corridor was filled side to side and as far as he could see with zombies.

The boy had climbed back to his feet and took off in a limping, awkward gallop as he moved away from them. "Run, you idiots!"

Bolivar stepped back from the door. He looked at Aben. "They're all dead."

One glance into the tunnel was enough for Aben. "Come on!" he said to Bolivar.

But Bolivar lagged behind. He could see them in there. Thousands of them. It reminded him of the Wells Fargo Center all over again. He couldn't allow that to happen.

"We have to get this door closed."

Aben shook his head, his wild hair flying. "No. We need to go. Now, Bol!"

"What numbers did you enter?" Bolivar hit the keypad. Nothing happened.

"I don't know. It wasn't me, anyway. That kid must have opened it from the inside."

The inside? The zombies were within fifteen yards now. One faster monster loped ahead of the pack. Bol stepped into the tunnel.

"What the hell are you doing? Get out of there!"

Bolivar searched for a way to close the door. He saw the key card slot. Where's the card? He searched the floor. Found it.

"Come on!" Aben jogged a few more steps away.

Bol grabbed the card off the floor and swiped it. The light stayed red. He tried again, but his hands shook. No dice. One more time, he thought. Third time's the charm.

Before he could make a third attempt, he felt the hand grab his shirt. Before he could react, teeth ripped through the material and sunk into his shoulder. He stumbled forward with an audible grunt.

Aben turned, saw what had happened. He ripped a pistol from a holster on his belt and shot. The first bullet missed. He shot again. That one hit the zombie in the cheek. It dropped, and Bolivar was free. Free but dead on his feet. He saw Aben moving toward him and motioned him back as he took out his own pistol.

"No! I'm bit. Go!"

"Shit! Fuck! Are you sure it got you?"

Bol reached back and came away with a palm wet with blood. He held it up for Aben to see. "Get the others out."

"I will."

Aben slid his gun across the floor to Bolivar, who grabbed it. He held a pistol in each hand.

"Thanks. And Aben?"

Aben looked to him. He could see more zombies nearing Bolivar's back. They were only a few feet away. "What?"

"Get a damn haircut. You're a disgrace."

Bolivar gave a pained smile. Aben's was weak, but he tried to return it. He raised his hand and gave a quick salute. Bolivar nodded, then turned to face his fate.

Between the two pistols, Bolivar had twenty-four rounds. He killed fourteen zombies with the first twenty-three shots, and by that time, they were upon him. The tunnel was filled with them. Packed in like sardines, he thought. I always hated sardines.

The monsters surrounded him, clawing and scratching and biting. One of them grabbed hold of his ear, and he felt the skin stretch, tear, then rip free from his head. Hot blood gushed from the wound.

Bolivar felt himself being ripped apart. The agony of hungry, undead mouths biting pierced deep into his body. He heard the fabric of his shirt tear and felt the cool, stale air of the tunnel against his belly. That feeling was replaced by hot blood flowing as the zombies tore open his abdomen.

Their hands reached inside of him, pulling out his intestines, ripping away organs. He thought of the others. He felt the worst about Grady. He'd promised he'd watch out for him.

His vision went black, and he knew the end was close. With the end came reanimation. He wanted that even less than death.

He managed to lift the pistol one more time, pressing the barrel under his chin. As he squeezed the trigger, he prayed the monsters took their time eating him and gave everyone else a chance.

CHAPTER FORTY-SEVEN

When Mina awoke, her body was pressed against the cool glass of the ambulance's windshield. She was contorted on its side, one foot tangled in the steering wheel.

How did I get here? What happened?

She opened her eyes, and everything was dark. It took a moment for them to adjust. When they did, she saw nothing to cure her confusion. Where was the road?

"You really did it now, Birdie. Got yo'self in a big old bind," her daddy's voice said.

She craned her neck to look out the windshield and saw nothing but brown mud. Her nasal passages burned. Is that smoke?

Mina knew something terrible had happened. The details didn't matter. Nothing mattered until she could find Bundy.

She freed her foot and rolled to face the opposite direction. She saw him there, suspended in his seat and held fast by his seatbelt. His head sagged, and she thought he looked like an oversized, lifeless doll.

No, that can't be. He has to be alive.

"Killed another one, Birdie. Seems like every man around you ends up dead."

Shut up, you old bastard! she thought as she crawled across the dashboard.

"Hey. Hey, handsome. Wake up. Come on." Mina used her fingers to open an eye. She saw his pupil contract. She breathed a little easier. Then he coughed, and his eyelids fluttered on their own. "That's good. That's real good."

He came around slowly, but that was fine. He was alive.

"Are you okay?" He slurred his words.

"I'm just fine. Don't you worry about me." She grabbed his hand.

"What about Peggy?"

Shoot, she'd forgotten all about the other woman in the ambulance. "Typical Birdie, only care about yo'self."

Mina peered into the rear of the ambulance, which was a dark cave aside from two rectangles of white where sunlight came in from above. "Peggy?" No answer came. She found her tossed ass over head, her body twisted and horribly askew.

"Damn it."

"What? Is she—" Bundy asked from behind her.

"Her neck's broke."

A thud rocked the van. Mina spun around and saw that Bundy had released himself from the belt and fallen against the dash. He groaned and rolled onto his back.

"Get out."

"What?"

"Get out of here before she turns."

Mina searched the floor for a gun, but everything had been upended in the crash.

Bundy pushed her into the back of the ambulance. "Go!"

It was eight feet to the rear door. Mina clawed her way along, but she was having little luck. She glanced back and saw Bundy emerging from between the front seats. "Get your butt back here and give me a push, big fella."

"I'm coming, boss."

She felt him behind her, the warmth of him against her back. He took her by the waist and raised her with as much ease as if he was lifting a pillow. Mina grabbed the door handle and threw it open.

Sunlight flooded into the rear of the ambulance, and she saw Wim peering down from above. Bundy lifted her higher, and she climbed free.

"What did I hit?"

"Nothing," Wim said. "The road's washed out. How are Bundy and Peggy?"

Shoot, she kept forgetting about Peggy. "Peggy's dead. Bundy's on his way."

She looked into the ambulance and saw Bundy attempting to pull himself the length of the box. He was red-faced and struggling.

"Are you gonna make it?"

Bundy was huffing, out of breath. "Aw, I'll get there. Just takes me a little longer."

Mina turned back to Wim. "Can you come down and help him, Wim?"

Wim nodded. "Sure thing. Ramey's getting a rope."

"Okay."

"Wim's coming. He'll get you ou—" She lost her words when she saw Peggy coming back to life behind him. The woman tumbled onto her side, into a sitting position. Her head lolled sideways, and her eyes set a target on Bundy.

BUNDY COULDN'T FIND his pistol. Couldn't find any of the guns he'd gathered together the last few days. He needed to put Peggy down before she reanimated but had no means of doing it without a firearm.

It was a nagging reminder of Mead insisting guns were poor choices. Maybe the little bastard was right after all. Bundy had nothing, not a knife or a hammer or even a damn brick. His only hope was escaping the ambulance before Peggy woke up.

He attempted to climb out of the box, but it took less than thirty seconds before he realized the pointlessness of that plan. He saw Mina looking down at him. The sunlight backlit her head, and she seemed to glow. Like an Angel, if he believed in such things.

"Wim's coming. He'll get you ou—"

Bundy saw her eyes grow wide. He had a good idea what had caused it, and he looked over his shoulder. Peggy had woken from her not-so-eternal slumber and was on the move.

He kicked back with his foot, catching her in the chest and tipping her over. She didn't stay down long. In seconds, she was back on her feet. He kicked out at her again, but this time, it was only a glancing blow. She caught his pant leg in her hands and pulled it toward her mouth.

She was inches away from sinking her teeth into his exposed calf. He could think of only one option. He let his body go limp and dropped down on her with all of his five hundred pounds. Beneath him, Peggy's body broke and burst.

Above, Mina's screams drowned out all other sounds.

He felt his head swimming, and he shook his noggin to clear it. He saw that Mina had dropped to her hands and knees, and half of her torso was extended into the box.

"Are you all right?"

Bundy looked around him. There was so much blood. "I'm not sure."

"Did you get bit?"

"I don't think so." He maneuvered himself through the pile of gore from what had once been Peggy and tried to bend his leg to check for bite wounds. That action was interrupted by a lightning bolt of pain that stretched from his leg, all the way into the pit of his stomach. He looked down and saw a bone jutting from his shin. Blood gushed from the wound.

"Well, shit."

"What? What is it?"

Bundy looked to her again. He saw Wim above her. Wim was looking at him, too. He had a coil of rope in his hands.

"We'll get you out of there, buddy. I'm gonna toss this down. Tie it around your waist."

Bundy appreciated the offer, but he was smart enough to know that this was game over.

CHAPTER FORTY-EIGHT

Juli heard the footsteps before she saw who they belonged to. They sounded awkward. Step, drag, step, drag. It sounded like a zombie. Earlier, Aben had given her a revolver. He had even taken her behind the hotel and set up empty cans for her to shoot at. She'd missed them all.

"Good thing a zombie's head is bigger than a soup can," was all he'd said about that.

She took the gun from her pocket and examined it, trying to remember how to use it. She flicked off the safety. Then what? She pulled back the hammer. That's all there is to it, she thought. Aside from aiming—that was the hard part. She stood at the ready as the source of the sound closed in.

What emerged wasn't a zombie. It was a teenage boy who ran with a limp. He appeared on the verge of collapsing. Juli lowered the revolver.

Mitch waved her away. "Get out of here. Everyone in the bunker is dead. And they're coming."

Juli couldn't believe her ears. "There's really a bunker?"

Mitch nodded. "I've been trapped in there for days."

More footsteps thundered against the tile. These were faster, and the boy glanced back, panicked. "Listen, lady. There's thousands of the fuckers! Go!"

"Did you see anyone else? Two of my friends are somewhere in the basement."

The teen didn't answer. He moved past Juli, who lingered. She couldn't help herself; she had to see what was coming. She almost raised the gun again, but Aben emerged.

"Aben! There was a boy! He said—"

"Zombies." Aben was out of breath and struggled to expel words. "Got Bol."

"What? No!"

"Got to get my dog. You get the dad."

He grabbed her hand and dragged her along. Juli looked back one final time. The floor vibrated underfoot. She couldn't see the zombies, but she could hear them coming. Like a stampede of wild horses in the distance.

By the time Aben and Juli had gathered Grady and the dog and made it outside, the horde of zombies was close enough that they could smell them. The kid, who had said his name was Mitch, hung around them at the periphery, and Aben noticed he'd helped himself to a pistol and a rifle.

"You know how to use that?"

Mitch looked from the rifle to Aben's face. "I've watched enough movies to figure it out."

With his remaining hand, Aben pointed to the rifle. "Fires better when the bolt's closed."

"Bolt?"

Aben reached over, grabbed the bolt, and closed it.

"Thanks."

"Thank me by not shooting one of us."

He thought the little prick sneered, but he had better things to worry about. Aben whistled for the dog, and it sprinted ahead of them and jumped into the backseat. Juli moved toward the passenger side.

"No!"

She looked up, startled.

"You drive."

"Me?"

He held up his stump. Might as well get some use out of the damned thing. She nodded and got behind the wheel.

Aben saw Mitch staring toward the Greenbrier. He had an idea why but looked anyway. Yep, that's what he had expected. The zombies were coming.

The creatures teemed out of the front entrances and into the courtyard. They spilled into the grass and gardens, smashing the almost endless carpet of red tulips underfoot. To Aben, it looked like they were running through a sea of blood.

Aben fell into the passenger seat. Juli already had the engine running. "Hit it," he said.

She did. She made a hard and fast u-turn that threw them back and forth in their seats. The car skidded into the grass for a moment, took out another swath of tulips, then she pulled it back onto the drive and pressed the pedal to the floor.

The tires gave a short squeal as they fought for traction, and then the Cruze leaped forward. Aben leaned out of the window and watched the hotel and the horde of zombies shrink in the distance. When they exited the resort property and hit the main street, Juli looked to him.

"Where are we going?"

It was a reasonable question. One for which he had nothing resembling an answer. "Damned if I know."

"Start with right or left."

He looked both ways. "Which direction did we come in from?"

"Left."

"Then turn right."

She did.

CHAPTER FORTY-NINE

After Ramey handed the rope off to Wim, she saw the zombies moving in the washed-out pit. It was more than she'd ever seen in one place at one time, and, to her, it looked like they were swarming.

They moved toward the ambulance, but blocking their way was a jumble of trees that was packed in tight and rose to the top of the crevasse. When the zombies reached it, the first row became entangled in the debris, but the others kept coming. They climbed atop their fallen, undead brethren and worked their way upward, out of the hole, nearing the destroyed highway.

"Wim."

Wim was busy looking into the ambulance. He had dropped the rope downward, where Mina fed it through the open door.

"Wim."

The first zombies escaped the pit. Only four, but more were coming. They clawed their way to freedom and moved toward the survivors.

"Wim! They're out!"

Wim looked over, his face confused, but that confusion gave way to dread when he saw what Ramey was shouting about.

"Good God almighty."

Ramey pulled her pistol and shot. The lead zombie fell. She shot again and missed completely. If they made it through this, she promised herself she wasn't going to stop practicing until she could kill these bastards every time she fired. But for now, she had to make do.

A third round took out a second zombie. More than a dozen had escaped. They were less than thirty yards away.

Wim looked down. "Bundy, hold tight. We have a situation at the moment." He reached toward Mina. "Give me your hand."

"No." She shook her head back and forth. "No. You get him out, Wim."

"You first, and stop arguing. There's a couple hundred zombies headed this way, so we gotta hurry."

"I said no!"

Ramey heard the rage in the woman's voice, but she was too busy shooting to give it much thought. Emory had joined her. He fired away with a revolver, but he was a much worse shot than any of them and was of little help. What a sad bunch of marksmen we are, she thought.

BUNDY HEARD the shooting and the subsequent panic in Wim's voice. Wim wasn't the type to panic unless the situation truly called for it, and that made up his mind.

"Wilhelmina," he said, and she looked at him, her eyes overflowing with tears. "Take his hand and go."

"I'm not doing that. I'm not leaving you."

"You have to. And do you know why?"

"Why?"

"Because I love you. And if I know you're gonna live, it's gonna be easier for me to die."

She wiped away the snot that ran from her nose. The waterworks were on full blast now. "You're not going to die!"

"I am. I got a busted leg, and I don't think you and Wim and Ramey and Emory combined could haul my fat ass outta here. Besides, it sounds like the gunfight at the OK Corral up there, and they've all got better things to do than waste time on me."

"Just stop it! Stop saying that."

After he did a full body drop on Peggy, Bundy had discovered a box he'd packed into the ambulance the day after they found the warehouse. It was something he and Mina had come across and hidden from Mead. Something he'd almost forgotten about.

"Do you remember why you said you liked me more than Mead?"

"What? No."

"Come on, think about it."

"I don't remember. And why's that matter now, anyway?"

"You said it was because you could outrun me. Well, baby, it's time to run." Bundy smiled, then looked past her to Wim. "Wim, get her out of here."

Wim leaned over the edge of the broken road. He had to stretch as far as possible to get anywhere near her. "Come on, Mina. Listen to him."

"Do it, Mina. Go."

"I don't want to."

"No, I imagine you don't. But we've both got to do something we don't want to do right now."

He opened the box and pulled out a stick of dynamite. Then he fished a lighter from his pocket.

"Say, how many zombies are out there, Wim?"

"A couple hundred."

Bundy let loose a low whistle. "A while back, Mead and I had a contest to see who could kill the most of those bastards. I'm pretty sure I'm gonna whoop his ass."

He felt Mina's tears fall onto his upturned face. He let them run into his mouth, enjoying his salty, final taste of her.

"I love you." Her words came out in retching sobs.

"Back at you, beautiful. You go on, now."

She turned away at last. He was so glad he didn't have to see her face anymore. Now, he could let his own tears flow. He watched her go. She needed to stand on her tiptoes before she could catch Wim's hand. She did, and he hauled her up.

She didn't look back as Wim ushered her away. Wim did look one last time, though. Bundy never thought a simple nod could appear to be a sad gesture, but that's what Wim did, and that's what it was. Bundy flicked the lighter and lit the fuse. "Take care of them, Wim."

"I'll do my best."

"That's all any of us can do."

Wim left. Bundy heard frantic voices as the gunshots stopped. He heard the Bronco's tires spinning against the asphalt and the sound growing quieter and quieter as it retreated.

Bundy sat the dynamite, with its blazing fuse, on top of the other twenty or so sticks that filled the box. He never got to use the explosives the way he had planned, but that was all right.

"Been a hell of a ride, boss."

He let his eyes fall shut. He had no desire to see what followed.

THEY WERE a mile away when the explosion shook the car. Wim looked in the side mirror and saw orange smoke drift upward, marring the blue sky.

He reached for Ramey. She took his hand between her own, raised it to her lips, and kissed his fingers. They didn't say anything. There weren't any words.

CHAPTER FIFTY

WIM DROVE NEARLY AN HOUR BEFORE HE FOUND AN ALTERNATE route. No one in the car had spoken a word. That changed when they stumbled upon a roadblock of abandoned vehicles.

Over two dozen cars and trucks covered the roadway. Even the embankments were blocked. Going around them would be impossible.

"What should we do now, William?" Emory asked.

Wim wasn't interested in being in charge, but it had happened by default. Wim stared at the jumble of cars, trucks, and SUVs. They hadn't passed more than five houses in the previous half hour, and Wim knew there was no way all these vehicles came together by chance. This was intentional. He opened the door.

"Let's stretch our legs."

Ramey slid out first. Wim followed. He watched the Bronco as Emory attempted to cajole Mina outside. Eventually, he did.

"Let me see that map again," Wim said to Ramey.

She pulled it from her back pocket, and when Wim unfolded it, he found the seams so worn that it was ready to fall to pieces. He tried to compare it to the route they'd taken, and, so far as he could tell, it matched up near perfect.

"It looks like there's a third way in, but it'll take us a few hours out of the way. Maybe more, depending on the roads."

Ramey watched him closely. He thought she could see through him like a pane of glass and tried to avoid her gaze.

"Wim? Are we there?"

Wim didn't answer. He tried to think of a decent fib, but before he could come up with one, a metallic clang on the pavement got his attention.

Ramey heard it, too, and they looked to see a canister not much larger than a soda can spewing a cloud of yellow gas. That was joined by four more.

Wim tried to grab Ramey, to get them back to the Bronco, but his head was foggy. He saw Mina fall to the ground. Then Emory.

"Wim?" Ramey called out, her voice sounding miles away.

His feet felt like they weighed a thousand pounds each, and he couldn't make himself move. He reached for Ramey, but he could no longer see her through the thick smoke.

He thought he heard something akin to heavy machinery, but before he could make a point to listen, the world went dark.

I'M SO COLD, Wim thought as he slowly regained consciousness. Why was he cold? The day had been hot. He felt like someone was pricking him over and over again with icicles.

His eyes fluttered, then opened. Everything was white. He thought that was due to the brightness and that his eyes hadn't adjusted yet, but as things came into focus, he saw white walls. A white ceiling.

He turned onto his side to avoid the icy assault. He saw a figure wearing, of course, white. Its face was hidden behind an opaque mask. The figure aimed a hose at him and something cold and wet, like water but with a chemical smell, rained on him.

As his mental fog cleared, he realized the person hosing him down was wearing a HazMat suit. He climbed to his knees, and when he did, he realized that he was naked. He tried to cover himself with his hands, and the person with the hose laughed.

"No need for modesty. I'm the one who stripped you down in the first place."

When he finished spraying Wim, the person handed him a towel. "Wipe yourself down good so that there's no residue. There's new clothes over there." He pointed at the corner, where clothing was folded in a neat pile.

The man left, and while Wim dried off, he wondered about the residue. He couldn't make sense of any of this. How did he even get here?

After he dressed, he moved toward a slit in the plastic wall through which sunlight spilled. Wim pushed at it and stepped into the open.

He saw two identical tents, but not the man with the hose. Or anyone at all. Parked nearby was an M-35 Cargo Truck with an open-air bed. He remembered the rumbling engine he'd heard in the fog and assumed that might be a match. But there was no driver. He decided to explore the area with the hope of locating his friends.

Wim found them clustered together a dozen yards away from a floating dock. In his glee to see his companions, he didn't give much thought to the dock or the lake beyond it. He barely noticed the motorboat tied off there or the man inside it.

Instead, he rushed to his friends. They all wore white drawstring pants and white cotton shirts, the same wardrobe Wim had been given. Ramey saw him approaching, and her face lit up.

"Wim!" She ran to him and threw her arms around his neck.

"Where are we?"

She shook her head. "I just woke up a few minutes ago. We all did." She ran her hand through his still damp hair. "You got a bath, too?"

"Yep. Not a very pleasant one, either."

She tried to smile but couldn't force one through the fear. Wim wanted to hold on to her and tell her everything was going to be okay, but he knew she'd see through that in a second.

He had no time to say anything because the man in the boat shouted. "Down here!"

Another man dropped over the hill behind them. He approached the foursome.

"This way, please." He ushered them toward the boat.

Wim hesitated. "Can you tell us what's going on?"

The man shook his head. "They'll give you more information at registration."

"Registration?"

The man didn't elaborate. "Climb aboard, friends. You're safe now."

Wim and Emory exchanged a skeptical gaze. Wim put his hand on Ramey's shoulder and squeezed it. He leaned in close to her ear. "I don't think we're in a position to protest."

"I think you're right."

The man on shore helped them into the boat. The driver gave them life vests.

"Safety first."

He flashed a warm smile. Once they all suited up, the boat took off.

Their journey by water took less than fifteen minutes. They reached another dock, where the driver tied up, then helped them step off.

Ahead, a sprawling, wooden wall stretched twenty-five feet into the air. A gate large enough to fit a tractor-trailer swung open from the top down, and it reminded Wim of a drawbridge without a moat.

Ramey leaned in close to him. "What the hell's going on?"

"I haven't the foggiest."

The boat driver pointed to the opening. "Head inside. Registration's to the left."

He sped away, kicking up a spray of water.

They trekked the twenty yards to the opening. When they passed through, they discovered what looked like a village.

Dozens of people tended to gardens, did construction on buildings, and went about life as usual. A few children dashed back and forth, tossing and chasing Frisbees. Wim even saw something that made his nerves almost disappear: chickens roaming freely and a half dozen pigs loitering about.

Registration was located inside a yurt. A middle-aged brunette with her hair pulled up in a bun stood inside and checked them in, asking their name, age, and home state. Ramey was up after Wim.

"Ramey Younkin. Eighteen. New York."

The woman looked confused or surprised. Wim couldn't tell which. She scurried to a man with a long gray ponytail, and they traded whispers. Wim tried his best to eavesdrop, but they were too far away.

As they finished their private conversation, the man made a beeline to Ramey. "Hello, Ramey. I'm Victor. Please, come with me."

Ramey held her ground. "No. I won't leave my friends."

The man chewed his lip, and Wim noticed he was rocking on his feet.

"How about you pick one?" Victor said.

Ramey chose Wim, and the two were whisked away. Emory raised his eyebrows as they passed. Wim shrugged his shoulders.

Once outside, Ramey demanded, "Tell me where you're taking us."

Wim didn't expect her to get an answer and was surprised when one came. "Nothing to be worried about. We're going to see Doc."

"Who's Doc?" she asked.

"He's our founder."

Victor didn't expound further because they stopped outside a small log cabin.

"Now what?" Ramey asked Victor.

He gave a wide, warm smile. "Go in. Doc's waiting for you."

He strolled away, leaving them alone. Ramey looked to Wim, unsure. "What do you think? Should we go in?"

Wim felt apprehensive about what laid behind the door, but the map had brought them all to this point. It was time to find out what really waited for them at the X. He nodded.

Ramey took his hand and pulled the door open. Together, they stepped inside.

The cabin was dark, despite two large skylights in the ceiling. Wim saw the shape of a man behind a large desk. A manila folder covered his face.

"Hello? They said you were expecting us," Ramey said, and Wim noticed a quiver in her voice he'd never heard before. It wasn't exactly fear, but it was close.

The man peered up, and a kerosene lantern cast yellow light onto his face. The first thing Wim noticed was a large, purple birthmark on his cheek. Its shape made him think of learning geography in elementary school. "Italy is the boot."

When Doc's face came into view, Ramey dropped Wim's hand. Doc broke into an ecstatic grin.

Ramey ran to him. "Daddy!"

They collided in an embrace. Wim heard her sobbing. He suddenly felt very much like a third wheel and tried to distract himself by looking around the cabin.

The walls were covered with maps and diagrams of chemical structures that might as well have been some alien language for as much sense as they made to Wim. He spotted a large calendar for the month of May. One day was circled in red, and the word "Philadelphia" was written inside it.

Wim remembered that date well. It was only two days before life on his farm ceased to exist. A shiver ran up his spine, but he tried to ignore it.

It seemed like hours had passed before Ramey and her father broke their embrace. When they did, the man wiped the tears from her eyes with his fingertips. "Oh, Ramey," he said. "I was so worried."

Ramey composed herself, at least somewhat. "I was, too. I thought you were dead. Like everyone else."

"Your mother?"

Ramey gave a quick nod.

"I'm so sorry. So, so sorry, Ramey. But I'm glad you're here. This makes me happier than you could ever imagine."

Ramey turned to Wim. "Wim brought me to you. He saved my life."

Her father strode toward him and shook his hand. His grip was firm, but Wim thought his hand clammy. "A million thanks to you. Wim, is it?"

Wim nodded. "Thanks aren't necessary. Your daughter is more than capable of taking care of herself. She had little choice, being left alone."

Doc flinched, a tic so quick it could have been easy to miss, but Wim noticed, and he was glad.

"She's a resilient girl. Always has been." Doc turned back to Ramey. "Let me show you both around."

He led them out of the cabin and into the common areas. He showed them a schoolhouse, several small gardens, even some dairy cows. He pointed out a few dozen small houses. "Less than half are occupied at present. We're hoping to bring in others. I heard there were four in your party?"

"There were more at one point," Wim said.

Doc didn't acknowledge that comment. As he showed them a communal dining room, Ramey cut him off.

"Daddy, what is this place?"

Doc smiled. Perhaps Ramey found the look to be joyful, but Wim saw something else. To Wim, Doc's smile held the weight of a man who'd just won a war. His eyes were full of pride, and when Wim got another shiver up his spine, he didn't ignore it.

Doc reached over and pushed a lock of Ramey's hair off her face. Like he wanted her to have a good look at what he had created.

"This is the Ark. This is where the world starts over."

Made in United States
Troutdale, OR
12/07/2023